Dedalus Original Fiction in Paperback

PRIMORDIAL SOUP

Christine Leunens was born in Hartford, Connecticut, the daughter of an Italian mother and a Belgian father. Her grandfather was the Flemish artist Guillaume Leunens. After graduating from the University of North Carolina at Chapel Hill she went to live in Europe with the intention of becoming a writer but ended up a fashion model, working for Givenchy, Pierre Balmain, Paco Rabanne, Nina Ricci and making tv commercials for Mercedes-Benz, Suzuki and the House of Fraser.

Her success enabled her to give up modelling for horse breeding in Picardy, where she wrote her first play in French, *Tu N'As Qu'A* and her second *Porcelain White* in English. She received an award from the Centre National du Cinema for her screenplay *Maux D'Amour.*

Christine Leunens now lives in Normandy and combines writing film scripts and fiction with the occasional modelling job.

Christine Leunens

Primordial Soup

Dedalus

To François Ivernel

Published in the UK by Dedalus Ltd, Langford Lodge, St Judith's Lane, Sawtry, Cambs, PE17 5XE

ISBN 1 873982 19 4

Dedalus is distributed in the United States by Subterranean Company, P.O. Box 160, 265 South Fifth Street, Monroe, Oregon 97456

Dedalus is distributed in Australia & New Zealand by Peribo Pty Ltd, 58 Beaumont Road, Mount Kuring-gai, N.S.W. 2080

Dedalus is distributed in Canada by Marginal Distribution, Unit 102, 277 George Street North, Peterborough, Ontario, KJ9 3G9

First published by Dedalus in 1999

Typeset by RefineCatch Ltd, Bungay, Suffolk
Printed in Finland by Wsoy

A C.I.P. listing for this book is available on request.

CHAPTER 1

"Eat, you!"

"But it won't go down . . ."

"You jus' put in de mouth an' swallow!" my mother yelled.

I added another finger width of leprosy-stricken banana into my mouth and wished she'd stop staring at me like that. It joined the stagnant reserve which I moved from right to left to show her I was trying.

"I don' wan' to see de cherry."

"De cherry," to which she alluded was the pouch for storing unwanted nutrition in my left cheek. She seized it and twisted until the saliva-softened food seeped back onto my palate.

"How long i' take?"

"I'm chewing."

"You wan' I count three??"

She had concluded there was nothing to chew. Leprous pus could, according to her logic and the laws of physics, slide down any inclined surface with ease. I wished it were the kitchen sink tube and not my own.

"One. Two . . ."

I drove my finger into the flesh and began to carve out the soft brown spots someone had the big idea to name bruises, all the while trying my hardest to stop imagining the banana was Mir'i·am's forearm and what I was sapping were the undrained sores under her scabs. What I considered a bruise, my mother considered consumable flesh. The banana was drawn out of my hand and thrown in my face, which I turned aside in time.

In less than a week, I could not walk straight any more than could a drunken sailor. I complained to my mother about it; she measured my legs, told me to eat more. I was carrying in groceries, when I fell down and chipped my front tooth on the driveway. She left the papaya, the fennel and the half-priced bags of whole-wheat flour where they were, and checked my polio vaccinations.

The doctor pressed my tongue with an ice-lolly stick, examined my eyes and ears with a ray of light. He told me to be still and with a fine pointed tool, pulled something yellowish out I thought was dried pus.

"How in hell did banana get in her ear?!" Most eyes squint with anger; Dr. Kreushkin's opened wide, exposing the upper pink edges of the lower eyelids that have always reminded me of ham.

"Oh, she do anyting, dat child, no' to eat her food. She'll make me ol' b'fore my time."

My mother shrugged, then readjusted the tissue paper in her cleavage. The beads of sweat on her lip, for some reason, bothered her less. Dr. Kreushkin looked down at me with unconcealed disgust. With a crinkle of the chin, I swallowed my pride. I was not allowed to contradict my mother, which basically meant, to tell the truth.

On our way home, she stopped at Mr. Walter's garage sale and purchased "Fool's Stool" for one dollar. Mr. Walter had designed it for his son, Jade, long before he was the local weather forecaster. "FOOL" was written on the seat with tenpenny nails, points up. My mother declared that from now on, until I cleared my plate, I would have to sit on it. She was a persuasive woman, and more often than not I ended up giving in.

Abandoned at the table, I was facing or rather faced by, a stuffed stag's head, and that, for hours on end. My father had eaten the rest of his forest-roaming body long ago in his bachelor days. The nails poked at my bottom until I lifted up one cheek after the other. Despite his imposing antlers, the stag had wise, benevolent eyes, like the suspended man we saw at Saint Andrew's on Sunday, whose open sores would save me from my sins.

"This is the body of Christ," explained our priest, and afterwards offered us some, "and this is the blood of Christ," which we were not obliged to drink, though my mother grudgingly gave up a nickel or a dime so he would drink it out of his golden chalice instead of us. At our father's funeral, my sister and I were each given a one inch figurine of the same man to hang around our necks on fine silver chains. I hid mine inside my dress. He was half-naked, and bleeding badly.

I think it is necessary to add that whenever my sister and I fought, my mother would throw her hands into the air and sob, "You own flesh an' blood! Flesh an' blood!" She repeated this phrase until, without quite seizing its meaning, the thought of my own sister as red meat made me cry as well. I would hug my sister and let her play with my Mr. Potato Head. The intensive doses of theology and genealogy did not assist my cold-blooded eating of flesh.

One evening, I was facing the stag who not only understood but granted me eternal salvation for not eating a quail that my mother had anointed with butter before baking, then baptized with whisky before setting aflame. In my mind, I called it Saint Quail, to join that space between purgatory and heaven that God reserved for Noah's faithful pairs. There it would find Lassie and Flipper from the original series, I was sure. Stag Head agreed in silent majesty, upon which Ursula Tatta rang the doorbell and let herself in.

"I'm fed up! Up to here!" she saluted her hair-line.

Before my mother asked for particulars, Ursula added, "With Harry."

That was how adults referred to Mr. Tatta, her bald-headed husband. My mother was relieved to see the bird on my plate as yet uneaten, and retreated with Ursula to the living room, a showroom of crystal ashtrays she would never consider offering anyone to use and carvings of more wounded men on crosses.

I pressed my ear to the door. From what I could understand, Ursula had not had dinner, Harry was drinking, and not at home, for she'd found matchboxes in his pockets when she did the laundry. There was a long silence before she admitted that she had smelt, "Harry's underwear."

I cracked the door open to see my mother holding Ursula in her arms, patting her back. I was ashamed that Harry had hurt her so. Had he neglected to wipe when he did a number two? I had sat sideways with my sister to share the toilet once and we began shoving for space then missed. My mother yelled but she didn't *cry* about it. I assumed it more forgivable with children.

That is when I learned the unspeakable circumstances of my own father's death. I had known that he was killed in a car crash when my sister was a baby and I, four. It had happened in Rhode Island, US21, when he was selling insurance policies for The Mutual Insurance Company of Freyburg, the tragedy rendering my sister and I fatherless, and my mother anaemic, or so I'd overheard.

"Paul," my mother began, Paul Lester was our father, "wasn' 'lone in de car."

Ursula stopped crying and stared at my mother in disbelief. "A woman?"

My mother played with one of the ashtrays, and for some time, there was no change in her expression. "All men are jus' animals," she finally responded, "dey think wit' wha's b'tween deir two legs."

"But how can you be sure that they were . . . " Ursula could not come up with a suitable verb.

"B'cause whe' de firemen, dey go through de chassis an' find 'em, it was in her mouth," my mother spoke wryly.

Here, Ursula gasped and covered her own, as if she feared intrusion of a similar sort. What was in the woman's mouth?

"It was bitten right off. He die on de spot. She chok-ed on it, Peggy Summer, only a youn' girl, she was jus' sixteen," added my mother with no regret, but rather as if the Old Testament God had given the incident special consideration. My mother believed in a personalized God that punished those who trespassed against her, including any salesman who didn't give her a reduction when she found a defect in his merchandise, be it a blouse, a sofa, or a loaf of bread, yet never seemed to fear Him herself; her personalized God realized she lived in a hard world. What could the girl have possibly been eating? An adjutant brain? An inner leg? We were, I remembered, not allowed to eat in my father's nauseatingly new-smelling car.

My mind was racing, especially when Ursula concluded it was better for my father, my mother and the girl that way. My mother returned to evaluate my progress. I rushed back to Fool's Stool and poked the quail with my fork.

"Mom, I'm really not hungry!" I complained so she would not suspect all I'd been lucky enough to learn.

My hand was trembling. My mother stared at me for some time.

"It's a'kay," she patted me on the head, "Go an' play wit' you sis'er."

I ran to tell Cecilia everything.

CHAPTER 2

Cecilia and I were given dye-kits with which to colour eggs boiled in vinegar. My mother had been indifferent to my aesthetical pleas to purchase white eggs. She claimed brown eggs more "natur'l". In reality, they were five cents less.

Cecilia proceeded in a spontaneous manner, dipping the brown shell in traditional Easter colours, yellow, pink, sky-blue. I wanted to give each of our guests a more unique egg. A tricoloured German flag egg seemed suitable for Ursula. I dipped the thinner end in orange, then discovered to my dismay that there was no black in the kit.

"Black is not a colour," smirked Cecilia.

I kept the upper part orange and gave the lower part blue eyes and orange freckles, for Tommy Tatta's egg. Cecilia said this wasn't nice. Taking her advice, I dipped it in blue, and the whole egg turned a dreary smoky purple, more suitable for Hallowe'en.

"It looks like a sparrow's egg now," Cecilia consoled with a forged smile and a somewhat humid pat on my shoulder.

It was out of the question that our mother would let us have extra eggs for the flops. Those cracked from overboiling, with outgrowths of egg white, we had to put in our own baskets. I thought the whole ceremony futile. Even the fanciest Easter egg was nothing but a hard-boiled egg when you came down to it.

Lucy and Rosa Minsky sat on the grass in the backyard, their knees opening and closing in their dresses like butterfly wings. Tommy Tatta and Timmy Tatta, Ursula must have been inspired by the Little Drummer Boy when choosing their first names, amused themselves by throwing our pebbles into the canal to make them skip. As soon as the adults proudly emerged with their camera, the children ran towards the boat davits where Easter baskets were conspicuously hung. My feet shovelled the gravel as I walked. The hiding places were an insult to human intelligence.

I chuckled inside. It was their first Easter at my mother's. My mother wasn't about to allow us to have chocolate bunnies, although she almost hesitated at white chocolate this year, claiming white more natural than brown. Unlike egg shells. She nevertheless abandoned the stiffly standing bunnies on the health food shelf. My mother refused to "throw hard-workin' money out de window for dat junk". "Hardworkin' money", meant money that accumulated interest.

The boys emptied their baskets on the dock. I watched their faces. Besides a boiled egg, each basket contained a pound of dates, unshelled walnuts and dried figs. Easter bunny must have turned into a health freak. Tommy picked up his handsomest walnut and threw it at the canal. It skipped five times, which was his record.

Timmy prepared to surpass him, when his father slapped him on the ear. Tommy, in wailing how much he hated nuts, only attracted a slap of his own. Both boys had to say thank you, audibly, to my mother. It was easier for the children that hadn't been slapped.

My mother returned to the kitchen. Sharon and Ursula offered to help, probably wanting to discuss in greater depth Mr. Tatta's potty-training problem. My mother said it would ruin the surprise and ordered me to set the table. I put out my mother's most elaborate china, silverware and crystal, praying I would not have to sit next to Mr. Tatta.

I sat across from him. As we eleven tore apart our stuffed artichokes, my mother answering each compliment with "fresh from de tree", I contemplated Mr. Tatta. I could not believe that a full-grown man with a pot belly, a Timex watch and a wedding band was not yet potty-trained. Then again, his baldness gave him the look of an overgrown baby. I imagined him wriggling on his back, his legs in the air, as Ursula wiped his bottom, sprinkled talc upon it and secured a safety pin into his nappy. Sharon Minsky had trouble looking at him, too. I supposed Ursula had let her in on the secret and she was imagining the same thing I was.

My mother presented the main course as a Lithuanian speciality her mother had passed on to her before she died, like hers had to her. She lifted the silver dome to reveal bony brown bits of meat with prunes mixed in. My mother warned there were stones in the prunes, but said they had more flavour that way. I was with her when she was shopping, she had wanted the stoneless ones but they were forty cents more.

Mr. Tatta blushed as he stared down at his plate. Maybe he thought my mother was trying to tell him something.

"Prunes?!" protested Tommy.

"You should not criticize before you try. Remember 'Green Eggs and Ham'?" asked Ursula before adding with a defiant stare, "Yes I like them, Sam I Am?!"

"I won't like 'em in any house, with any mouse," Tommy broke off as his father's face foreboded another slap.

Cecilia gave thanks for this day, the sunny weather, our health, named each of us present, including "mōciùté" ("granny" in Lithuanian) already in heaven, then at last thanked God for the food we were about to eat. Stag Head and I exchanged a look of sympathy.

Everyone but me had dug in and was not unpleasantly surprised, when Timmy had to go and ask what it was. He was too young to know that what you don't know doesn't hurt you. My mother straightened up, stuck her chin as high as it would go to make herself appear taller (a technique she resorted to whenever she saw her reflection in a store window or a camera was aimed anywhere near her) and proclaimed, "Rabbit."

"It's a great specialtay, rabbit," she bragged, "some German beer on de top and he cook wit' prune . . . I clean him myself, he was very young, very fresh, beautiful . . . "

Lucy and Rosa began to weep, followed by Tommy and Timmy.

Rosa, usually the quiet one, blubbered, "You mean we're *eating* the Easter bunny??"

My mother did not understand, "But it is Easter, no?!"

I guess she didn't quite pick up the difference between eating chocolate and living, breathing rabbits across the nation.

"We're eating the Easter bunny!!" confirmed Lucy, covering her face with her forearms.

The other children repeated this phrase endlessly, followed by funereal sobs. It was as if my mother had served Santa Claus on Christmas Day. Lucky they hadn't come over that Christmas Eve when she had made venison with cranberries, Rosa would have accused her of brewing Rudolf the Red-nosed Reindeer and the cranberries would have probably glowed.

Stag Head looked as though he bore the weight of the world on his plaque and his antlers already were heavy enough. Ursula kept on nibbling to make light of the matter, and as a member of the German-American club, she had probably already eaten worse in her knackwursts. Sharon contemplated her girls, afraid they would be traumatized. They had sheltered lives, they didn't have to live with my mother.

"Go eat what's in your baskets. You can go outside," Joseph Minsky advised.

"It's more than de Indians, dey have, dey should be tankful to me," retorted my mother when they were gone. She confused Easter with Thanksgiving.

"De more for us," she added, her feelings hurt, which basically meant leftovers for me.

The following day, I suffered upon Fool's Stool two hours before gnawing at Easter bunny's hind leg in Stag Head's company. I wondered if the land of milk and honey was a land of *only* milk and honey. I slipped off my sandals. They hurt my feet anyway. They would have to hurt more before I was given another pair.

CHAPTER 3

Ursula popped by regularly to see how we were doing at dinner-time. In the kitchen light, her sparse eyebrows gave a small sanctuary to the burgundy streak of eyebrow pencil. Her hair had recently been dyed to a pepper red, but the chlorine and the sun were robbing it of some vital element and it was turning into a burnt-looking burgundy. I noticed she always carried with her, even in an evening gown, a faint scent of suntan lotion. No one could compete with her tan; her forearm beat anyone who dared present their own next to hers, as I often did.

My mother slid lima beans into an iron pot of salted water. Ursula unwrapped a bundle of brown paper to reveal four forked hooves.

"Pi' feet, oh!!" my mother laughed merrily.

The skin was rubbery and thick, the colour of the Crayola crayon called "flesh".

"My grandparents used to eat the tail," admitted Ursula.

If mine did, I wouldn't go around bragging about it.

"But the butcher said he already threw it away. Would make good fishing, you should tell Joseph to stick one on his hook and toss it in your canal."

"We ask de butcher to save dem for us nex' time, I put it, you know, in my crab trap. I get stone crab wit' it, big, beautiful like dis . . . " I looked up quickly to catch my mother in the midst of a lie; her demonstration, honest to the point of vapidity, disappointed me: big was not bigger than her index and thumbs joining together to form a crab's spadelike back, which left three fingers on each hand to wiggle for the legs.

Ursula plopped the hooves into the steamy water.

"In honor of Harry," she dryly claimed.

Ursula used any pretext to swerve the conversation back to Harry. I thought she came over to forget Harry.

"He still up to such no-sense?"

"Oh, he denies it, but . . . " Ursula wriggled her nose emphatically, "I see it. I smell it. His collar's a classic . . . His britches . . ." Ursula stopped as she looked at me.

I pretended to play with a stray lima bean as if it were a car, producing a brr-brr noise I was too old for.

"From what I can tell, somebody out there's wearing 'White Linen', which I take as a personal insult because I'm sure she knows I'm the one doing the dirty laundry. *Pig*-dirty laundry!"

Ursula grabbed the lima bean I had momentarily parked on the kitchen tile and flung it down the garbage disposal.

"What's linen?" I asked when the grinding had stopped.

"Go set de table, you!" snapped my mother, "Don' always stick you big nose inside ot'her people's oats!"

I was about to remind her that one can say "business" or "bee's wax" but not "oats", but the look on her face told me it was not the best time. If any human soul thinks they are going to persuade me to eat a pig hoof, they are making a big mistake, I muttered to myself.

Each time I returned to the kitchen, I caught fleeting bits of conversation. Harry was working all the time. He worked on weekends. He worked late at night. He went on business trips to Tallahassee. I guess being an estate agent was demanding, especially in a growing area like Cypress County. I felt sorry for Mr. Tatta. Just for that, Ursula was considering leaving him.

"Take wha' you can get, you," my mother offered Ursula her own slogan in life, both pecuniary and spiritual.

"Yuck!" exclaimed Cecilia when Ursula clarified for what exactly she was about to say grace.

My mother gave me the evil eye. I suppose she thought Cecilia had learned the word from me. I stabbed one lima bean after another. Black-eyed beans were Cyclops, but lima beans were eyeless and reminded me of something a caterpillar would gnaw its way out of. Ursula, trying to carry on the kitchen conversation, spelled every other word, but my mother was having trouble with the English spelling. Ursula didn't speak Lithuanian. My mother didn't speak Pig Latin.

My mouth was packed with the putrid flesh of the hoof. Too repulsed to resort to "de cherry", I brought the napkin to my face, and out of true desperation, narrowed my lips and blew it out, hoping the sound resembled someone sneezing. My napkin bloated. Ursula cringed.

"Mótina! Can't she go to the bathroom to do that?" urged Cecilia, adding again, "Yuck!"

This time she was pinched for it.

I dropped the napkin in the toilet and as soon realized my error. A film of finely chopped pink expanded over the water surface and remained stagnant and unsightly. My mother lived as though we were in some European war. In the United States, in a time of prosperity, she cut paper napkins in two, forbade reading at night, and would not let us go in and out of anywhere, the refrigerator, the house. The temperature could rise one degree and it took energy, thus hardworking money, to cool it down. Flushing the toilet more than once a day made her scream, "You don' use twenty litres for jus' a teeny yellow water!"

It wasn't like we were poor. We lived on the water. My mother had two jobs, making her money work and full-time penny-pincher, both of which she took seriously. Trembling, I filled the waste can with water and thrust it into the bowl like I had seen my mother do to change the water in her toilet that she used as a bidet to save water during the week. She was stealing lima beans from my plate as I returned to the table. I slowed down before she saw me.

My cold lasted some time. To make it more realistic, I sneezed between meals, too, and had occasional coughing fits. I shouldn't have overdone it. Doctor Kreushkin checked the thermometer and glued his palm to my temperate forehead. I, in most likelihood, let my eyelids sag much more than they really would for a common cold. Doctor Kreushkin lifted them and examined my normal pupil dilation.

"Wha' is it??" my mother questioned, worried his silence signified disease.

"I suspect . . . Could be allergies . . . "

"Allergies?" my mother's voice rose, as though it were his fault. Allergies sounded expensive to her. She would argue her way out of it. "Her nose! It is a'ways full! I give her fresh squeeze orange juice! I keep her from de school! An' still, her nose is a'ways full! De poor chil', her ears, dey hurting her! Now you do sometin'!"

My mother always forgot to say "please". Doctor Kreushkin tried to explain how disturbances of the respiratory tract could be due to many different causes. I feared my mother would explode any minute.

"I'm feeling better. Look." I jumped twice. "It's just a runny nose!"

"Keep quite, you! Nobody pays you!"

Dr. Kreushkin took offence. My mother threatened not to pay unless something more medically competent was done than putting his hand for five seconds to my forehead. Under pressure, he signed a prescription for antibiotics and told her to call him in ten days.

My mother had faith in the antibiotics. I had even gone so far as to get her to let me take them with chocolate milk. Cecilia reacted melodramatically over her not getting to have any.

"You sis'er is sick! You, be lucky you not sick!"

My over-confidence grew and God found my acquisitions dishonest, especially my first glass of Coca-Cola. I took another piece of steak into my mouth and didn't even bother to chew. I was blowing it back out when suddenly God struck me with his wrath and ordered the Coca-Cola bubbles to ascend to His Kingdom in Heaven. The additional pressure unexpectedly ejected the meat through my half-napkin; it landed a few inches in front of me, next to my glass. My mother at first blinked at it in apprehension, as if this were the final stage of tuberculosis.

"Yuck!" exclaimed Cecilia, then she had to go and ask, "Did that come out of her *nose*?!?"

"Let me see dose ot'her napkin," my mother requested.

Next to my plate were a few balled-up ones I hadn't bothered to throw away. My lack of movement was confirming her suspicions. She reached over the table. As she opened her valuable half-napkins up, one after the other, each contained, to her horror and to Cecilia's fascination, a piece of steak. Crying, my mother called the flesh I'd wasted, "her own sweat an' blood". I was lost in confusion.

Locked up in the pantry closet, I stared at the shadows of hanging prosciutto with distaste. A silhouette of provolone cheese in a nylon net swayed in the air as I hit it with a yardstick. I was seated on a twenty pound bag of Idaho potatoes. The stale air reeked of smoked carcass, thyme, nutmeg, goose-garlic and onion-chive. It wasn't as if I hadn't been offered a choice. I could have gone to my room, but there I would have had to write, "I will not in the futur I pramice, to spit Momy's hardworking meet out of the window." I found the phrase long for five hundred times, even if I had already convinced her to scratch off the redundant "never again". I could have stood outside with one foot on Fool's Stool, but I wasn't keen on Ursula seeing me like that, should she come over. At least here, I could play.

"The *closet*?? Geez! Isn't that kind of . . . severe? Locking up your daughter in a *dungeon*?" I rejoiced at Ursula's shocked tone.

"Dere's no lock!" replied my mother, "an' she deserve."

"Yeah!" added Cecilia, "That's what she gets for trying to fool us."

"Us" . . . I vowed to myself that I would tell my mother to look under Cecilia's bed. She had broken my mother's Greatest of Modest Moussorgsky record thinking it could soar like a Frisbee and thought it had less chance of being noticed there.

"You! Go to bed! It's pas' you time!" accused my mother.

"No it's not!" retorted Cecilia who could not quite read Roman numerals, yet had fine intuition when adults wanted to be alone.

"You wan' go wit' you sister in de closet?" threatened my mother.

I hoped she would say yes, but hearing no answer after a while meant she preferred the comfort of her bed. I shifted the potatoes more comfortably under my bottom and tried to sleep.

Suddenly, I heard something rustle, probably my own foot, scratching a stem of bay leaves. Cockroaches darted into my mind. I imagined them by the dozens, feasting on the mounds of organic reserves. If I hadn't had sandals on, it wouldn't have been so bad, but my mother was convinced that our feet should "breathe".

"Mom! I've got to urinate!" I shouted.

In our household, we were allowed to use the noun but not the verb "pee".

"Mom!" I yelled louder, slapping my arms and feet anywhere I felt the scrunchy little legs were likely to creep.

My mother opened the door, allowing a ration of the kitchen light to peer in. To my surprise, the pantry looked exactly like I had found it.

"Jus' be quick," she warned, as her top lip curled in enough so that one could see her gums above her teeth.

On my way to the bathroom, I had noticed a red suitcase. The metal clip "Samsonite" confirmed my hunch, my mother would never pay extra for a famous brand name and even I had seen an ape jump on one of these on TV. Was

Ursula going to live with us? Would she have some influence on my mother, who didn't know American justice? Someone turned off the kitchen light and the last rays that had comforted me through the gap under the door were gone. I blinked into the darkness.

I pretended I was Anne Frank to make the time go by. I imagined sharing the space with Ursula, Harry, Tommy, and Timmy Tatta, having to live on small portions of bread, sleep together on the floor and drink broth out of the same thermos. I was still young and naive enough to think it sounded fun. But the dark tampered with my imagination and I grew unspeakably bored. My sweat trickled down my chest in small rivulets. I wished I were allowed to at least flip through the pages of a cookbook, but my mother would not invest in unnecessary wattage after the doctor's bill. When I had meekly asked her when I could come back out, she only replied, "Whe' I feel like. You deserve all night."

My fingers throbbed after I broke through the net to procure an Idaho potato. I held it in my palm. The outside felt dusty and cold. With my fingernail, I scratched off the eyes and clumps of dirt. Mrs. Wella, my fifth grade teacher, said that a raw potato turned to starch then to sugar in your mouth after awhile. She had told us to experiment with this at home, but my mother had refused to spare a potato for "such stupidity". I bit through until I came upon a skinless bite. I churned it in my mouth, expecting to discover the taste of candy. Waiting for the potato to transform seemed longer than for my mother to show up, and less likely.

I knew my mother came from a country like Alice in Wonderland's rabbit-hole, where heads used to be chopped off and those who managed to keep theirs watched like we watch cartoons on TV. But still, this was the United States. Even if people in Japan have rooms smaller than this, in this country we call it a "closet". I could see my mother in her recliner, her feet up at a forty-five degree angle, chatting with

Ursula as she sipped a salt-rimmed martini and dipped her hand in a bowl of pistachios. How peaceful she must find the evening without a child butting in to ask a question. Maybe she'd decide to keep me here until I was old enough to support myself. I'd be blind by then, mute, wrinkled; a vegetable . . . I cried louder than I normally would have, hoping someone out there might come to my rescue or at least feel bad.

The doorbell rang.

"Who's dere?!" my mother never failed to consult the peeping hole before asking.

"Harry. Who the devil do you think?! The Ambassador of Vilna??"

"A' dis time of de night?" My mother's aggressiveness was already thinning.

The screen door screeched. I sighed. Some men knew how to handle my mother. Their bark had to be louder than her bite. My mother encouraged Ursula, Ursula insulted Harry, Harry laughed at Ursula's silliness before repeating "Goodnight" and "Thanks a million" to my mother. I knew she would soon be on her way. I lay tragically on my stomach with droopy, eagle-spread arms, like Ulysses cast upon the shore without drink for ten days.

When I awoke, my back was stiff. My hair dripped over my neck like seaweed off an uplifted anchor. Potatoes were pushing into my chest and my foot was stuck under a bottom shelf, next to a soldier line of unopened family-sized dill pickles. There must have been a liquidation sale.

"Can I come out now?" I would walk straight up to my mother and ask in a simple, direct manner; yet I procrastinated. She would be capable of doubling the sentence if she considered it an impudence.

I tiptoed down the corridor. To one side, was an ancestral portrait in oil. A man on horseback wore a handlebar moustache that only a Hell's Angel would be caught dead wearing today. It ran into the low ceiling, where the cavalier's throat was nearly sliced by the fan's blades. I assumed it had once belonged to my father.

On the opposite wall were my mother's two attempts at art. "Sun, Sky, and Tree" looked more like "Bacon and Egg" because the sky was white and dominated by the yellow globe; and the tree, a trunk without branches, was brick red. "Self-portrait of the artist" was but a circle painted on a square and what were supposed to be earrings looked like golden fringed military shoulder-pieces, after all, there was no neck. One upside down triangle represented both her eyebrows. An orange slice represented her mouth, facing down. Signed Olga Yulof, her maiden name. Cecilia and I called it, "Mótina is watching you." It prevented evil spirits from getting anywhere near the house.

I could hear sheets stirring as I neared the door of her bedroom. My knees grew weak as I turned the knob. The sheets continued to rustle followed by occasional gasps for breath, as though she were dreaming that she was running in some race. I feared waking her, lest she was just steps away from victory. I strained to make out two acrobatic forms. One was obviously my mother, arching her back; her legs, bent and open, gave strange little jerks, as did her hips. The other seemed to be feeding gluttonously on her stomach. As it descended lower, my mother gave little cries of pain and struck his back a few times with her heel.

"Eat me . . ." I was startled to hear Ursula's voice and not my mother's.

I figured out that it must be Harry, who began to make slopping noises like when a dog laps water; his jaws and lips were without any doubt up to some strange work.

I covered my mouth, thinking I'd vomit or faint. I could tell from Ursula's groaning that he was hurting her. She took hold of his great bald head and tried to pull it back up. He refused. She stifled the sounds of her pain by biting a pillow. At Sharon Minsky's sister's daughter's wedding, the priest had proclaimed that man and woman will become one flesh. I hadn't understood what exactly that meant, though I had imagined the newly-weds united, not so much as a man and wife shish kebab but as a rosary, with pink and white beads touching each other as our own palms do in prayer. Were couples forced to consume each other's flesh? Or somehow share each other's meat?

"No, no, no . . ." protested Ursula . . .

Her voice had grown deathly weak, very much as though she had lost mouthfuls of flesh and blood; yet Harry continued to gnaw mercilessly at her thighs. The sounds he made were sickening me. How could anyone watch unmoved. I ran to the refrigerator, desperately sought my leftover steak that I finally found on the second to bottom shelf in the right Tupperware behind the leftover carrots and leeks, and rushed back to the bedroom.

Harry was now on top of Ursula, crushing her. He panted like a wild beast as he tried breast-feeding from both her breasts at one time. He squeezed them together with both hands like a bouquet and sucked. He was starving. Ursula threw her head from side to side in pain.

"Now!" Harry ordered her, shaking her repeatedly with his whole body to get her to react.

I switched on my mother's bedside lamp and bravely offered my cold meat to Harry, holding the opened Tupperware container as close as I could to his mouth.

Harry and Ursula stopped moving. Ursula's neck and breasts had red specks all over them. No wonder she was in pain, I thought. Harry's back had long scratches down it, some of which were bleeding. I started. Was Ursula defending herself or feeding on him, too? Well, they can both share my steak.

"Thank you, um, Kate, that'll do," Ursula pulled my mother's sheets up over Harry's shoulders.

Harry still hadn't moved but remained poised on his fists,

like a bulldog. Only his ribs continued to move, in and out, irregularly. His belly, hairy and drooping, never looked so huge.

"Thank you, Kate," Ursula repeated. I suppose I really was contemplating the last hairs that had not yet abandoned Harry's bald patch.

"Get lost, kid," Harry finally barked.

I was hurt, usually he called me "Sweetie."

Unable to think, I found myself returning to my own room. My mother was sound asleep in my bed, snoring softly. Appalled, I took back my Raggedy Ann and sock monkey and went to sleep on the sofa. But I couldn't sleep. Ursula had said, "Eat me." I'd heard it with my own ears. The priest had said, "Man and woman will become one flesh." Was my father being fed upon, too, when he was killed? The firemen had found "it" in sixteen-year-old "Peggy's" mouth.

Perhaps a fruit grows down there, I conjectured. An apple, that in God's punishment to Adam, every woman and man must still eat. Or a vegetable? I concluded it must be meat. Otherwise, why would the priest have distinctly used the word "flesh". Which meant it was raw. A sort of meat that probably kept growing back over and over again, like a fingernail. No wonder my mother kept forcing me to eat red meat. She was preparing me for adulthood.

CHAPTER 4

Cecilia stepped around the spray of every over-enthusiastic sprinkler, swinging her Miss America lunch box out in large arcs. I trudged along, my sighs turning into yawns. Well before dawn, the sound of my mother's heavy urination had warned me to return to the pantry closet. I'd hardly slept. When we got to the bus stop, Cecilia squatted, opened the hatch with the bathing beauties and took out crinkly aluminum paper packages. My mother actually hand washed aluminum paper, we always had to bring it back. She bragged a roll can last ten years. Not that we didn't have a dishwasher. My mother used it for storing lentils when they were on offer. She said washing dishes was easier by hand. And I suppose it was, since Cecilia and I were always the ones to do it.

As Cecilia undressed the aluminum forms to see what leftovers awaited her, I continued to ponder at what grown men could possibly lodge inside their trousers; and if that wasn't the reason they permanently wore belts, to keep hands and unwanted mouths outside. I knew "it" was what separated girl from boy, but I didn't know what "it" frankly was. Until then, I imagined it to be chain links. Unexpectedly, the chain links converted into sausage links. I almost laughed aloud, finding that utterly grotesque. Harry stood in front of a frying pan as they cooked, curling his toes into the floor. He faced Ursula with his dangling specialty. To his great pain, she ate them off, and they in this way became flesh united. But the sausages kept growing and Ursula grew sick of eating them. Maybe one grew per day. A man could not go walking around with a line of sausages trailing out of his trouser leg.

The school bus drove up with its familiar yellow snout. Cecilia and I were wearing narrow, scarlet gowns and had trouble stepping up, for the gowns cupped our ankles in their bottom rings of lace. Josh Kugel and Barry Ramsey cut across the corner lawn and pushed us aside.

"Out of the way, Mary Poppins!"

Barry was the meanest. I felt, though dared not inform him that he was ignorant. We were dressed not as Mary Poppins but Anna Karenina. In the United States of America, in the midst of the fanaticism for Levi jeans and corduroy trousers, Nike and Adidas trainers, Cecilia and I attended class in exorbitant gowns, inspired from I don't know what century but not the twentieth. To make it worse, my mother made Cecilia and me exactly the same model so we would not be jealous of each other.

My mother was kind enough to make us three versions of the same pattern so we could have a fresh dress to wear every other day, but it looked as though we were wearing the same dress all week. At school, we were baptized the Bobsey Twins. My mother could not understand our complaining. She had attended an all-girls Catholic school in Vilna and they wore uniforms. She'd only had one uniform all year, which she hand-washed with the soap they themselves made with their hardwork and sweat.

After putting up with puerile ammunition, spitballs and rubber bands, despite taking care to sit directly behind Mr. Ginger, the octogenarian bus driver who proved (purposely) deaf, dumb (and unfeeling; because of us, he was hit once in a while, too), Cecilia and I each went our own way. I hated walking past the bigger kids, leaning against the wall.

"It's Heinz ketchup! Hey! Heinz ketchup?!"

"*Supercalifragilisticexpialidocious . . .*"

The familiar Mary Poppins tune . . . I would never make a friend. I guess one generation has to do the melting before the others may brew less conspicuously in the pot.

"Frank Tudor. Kirk Gummer. Okay. Kate Lester?" Mrs. Wella checked off my name. Nowadays, I just signed instead of asking my mother to do so. It used to be that when she saw the statement about the school not being responsible if I was injured during an excursion, she refused to sign. I would be the only child to sit in an empty classroom with a substitute teacher, with pages of arithmetic problems to solve so she could write a love letter to her boyfriend.

We would watch two reels of a film in the morning, have lunch, then visit Coral Springs Zoo. That meant driving over Gables Bridge, which was cause for excitement. On top, we occasionally spotted porpoise and about once a year, it lifted to welcome a yacht into our bay.

Numbers flickered on the screen, ten down to one. A white haired man greeted us, presented a view of the earth seen from the moon, and asked us to follow a drop of water which evaporated to the notes of a harp. Then to a cymbal trying to sound like thunder, rain dropped over a rolling ocean. I wondered how they knew it was the same drop, but after awhile my arm grew tired and I put it back down. When we'd reached Antarctica, I recognized my mother's Wagner record. The crescendo went better with the pure, white vastness than it did with my mother's pebble-stone patio.

An icicle began to thaw and a drop fell, enabling daisies to grow. The camera closed in on a butterfly drying its wings on one, when a frog's tongue attacked the frail creature. The frog was ravaged by a snake, the snake in turn was seized by a pair of talons and wiggled its adieu to the camera below, as a falcon joined the horizon. The white haired man returned to explain.

"The food chain," he began.

I didn't feel well. Mrs. Wella put a new reel on the projector. I rose to sharpen my pencil. I ground it down to a stub, smelling the old and new shreds of lead and wood tossing around in an earthy mix.

"Sit down, Kate," ordered Mrs. Wella.

I stepped back to my desk in a trance, overcome by the drier sound of lions tearing the skin of some hoofed creature, quite like the raking of dead leaves off a driveway.

"Can you pick up the pace, Kate?" questioned Mrs. Wella.

The aisle before me turned into a stream I waded down, as fish dodged from me as they would a grizzly paw.

"Kate? Is everything all right?"

I heard some of the children laughing. It felt as if my brain were a small cork bobbing about the five oceans of the world. How fast must the hare flee so as not to wither into another? How high should the cricket leap? How pointed must horns be in order to fend off those who wish to eat us? I didn't want to be eaten. What defences would I have against grown men?

"Kate? Kate? Wake up!" I discovered a collage of worried faces peering down at me, including those who usually tried to trip me. My mind was soupy with confusion. I remember hearing myself repeat, "paradise lost".

"It's all Adam's fault," I wailed to Adam Freeman's dismay.

"Nu-uh! I wasn't anywhere near her!" he protested.

I continued, "If *he* hadn't bitten the apple, none of the animals ever would have started biting! Why should God punish us *all*?! It's not fair! It's not fair! I didn't do anything!"

Mrs. Wella seemed to catch on, but her face looked all the more worried. "Shh, now you just hush, darling . . ."

Dorothy told me to sleep. She was the school nurse, known to soothe the principal Mr. Liverpool's headaches. Contradictions, enigmas, frolicked in my mind. Do lions hate zebra? Then why do they eat them? If it is because they like zebra, why do they growl before pouncing? Why would they eat a friend? Does the zebra become the lion? Or does the lion become part zebra?

The sick room walls were silent, pink, except for a poster of a human silhouette with foodstuffs drawn inside. The slogan read, "You are what you eat." I wondered what adults were always trying to get at. If *I* were what I was forced against my free will to eat, then was I not already many living things? Wasn't I a turkey, a rabbit, part pig and cow by now?

"Boy, she's sure going to be disappointed not to visit the zoo this afternoon," I overheard Mrs. Wella in the hallway.

"Wha' zoo? Whose zoo?! I din' give permission to go to no zoo!!"

My heart jumped at the recognition of my mother's voice. Whenever she talked in public places, she assumed that everything she said was of great interest, and therefore spoke loud enough to share her wisdom with everyone present.

"I don' give hardworkin' money to Yuncle Sam so you drag my child to de zoo! I sen' my chil'ren here to learn! To b'come sometin' later in life!"

I hoped Mrs. Wella might promote the eminence of biology, but she referred back to the permission slip she was certain my mother had signed.

"Kate Lester. Mrs. Lester? Did you not sign this waiver?"

"Waiver of wha'!" accused my mother who when she did not understand something, converted rapidly into her pressure-cooker state of mind.

"A waiver of responsibility."

"Le' me see dat!"

I imagined my mother had just torn the slip out of Mrs. Wella's hand. I would never be able to face her again.

After a menacing silence, my mother shouted, "No! Me, never in my life, I sign dat!" in a tone of righteous indignation, as though Mrs. Wella was insinuating that she had, but now for some reason was trying to get out of it.

The door opened. I stopped breathing, yet my heart wouldn't slow down. In front of Mrs. Wella and Dorothy, my mother ordered, "De truth! You! You do dis?!"

What she was referring to was the forged scribble of her own signature.

In the meekest of voices I uttered, "I wanted, Mommy, just to be with the other ki . . . "

My explanation was interrupted by the impact of her palm. It wasn't a strong, impulsive slap, but she had the bad habit of doing it on the mouth and my front teeth had grown in at that unfortunate angle that made them buck.

One is always surprised in tasting one's own blood how similar its flavour is to the juice of a steak. I tried to push my tongue back into my throat so I could avoid the somewhat salty flavour, but there was no getting away from it. I wasn't wishing to be dramatic when I allowed, and somewhat helped, the crimson to dribble down my chin like baby-drool. Mrs. Wella's gasp weakened me. I found myself crying as audibly as a baby in front of her.

"Please, madam, don't be so hard on her, she's only a child . . . " Mrs. Wella only wished to help.

"You mind you own oats! Who pu' in a child's head to go to de zoo?!" inquired my mother, both fists on her hips. Mrs. Wella remained speechless. I believe she was afraid of being struck, too.

Meanwhile, Dorothy applied cotton to my wound, and then a bandage, which wasn't practical on a moist inner lip. She rolled her eyes at my mother's every word.

"You!"

It was now Dorothy's turn. Spending time with my mother meant there would be many places where you'd never want to go back.

"Such stupidity, never I see, to pu' a stupid ban'age on de inside of a lip! You! You go to school to learn dat?! Even a child, she know a ban'age, it will not adhere onto de inside of a lip!"

"I was just *trying*," retorted Dorothy with a sarcastic tone and a toss of her sleek blonde hair to the back, "is *that okay* with you??" She rolled her eyes again.

"You need try to know? Me, I don' need try to know, I *see*, I use my brains, see!"

At this, my mother indignantly lifted the bloody bandage out of my mouth and let it drop into the waste basket.

"An' you teach our chil'ren! Kate, honey, pu' you shoes back on."

"If it's true you see so well, you might have noticed I'm a nurse, I don't teach," retorted Dorothy on our way out.

My mother was holding my hand, which made me feel like I was on her side when I was strenuously trying to relax my facial expression to appear neutral.

"Tank Guard! Maybe dere is a future for our chil'ren, af'er all." My mother slammed the door so everyone in the hallway could share her exit.

CHAPTER 5

"Never, I can take my eye off you," repeated my mother.

It had become a musical phrase, as she went about her own kitchen business, lifting the steam-jingling pot covers and dropping them back down like cymbals.

"Never, I can take my eye off you . . . "

"Then why do you close the door??"

The short pause was to me a long stretch of hope, broken by another, "Never, I can take my eye off you," the sighing version.

I supposed even as a suggestion to crack open the pantry door, she wasn't about to give in. My mother wasn't that mad at me about the forged signature. After the number of "stolen" solitary diamond and ruby rings she had had converted into pendant necklaces before filing insurance claims, she wasn't one to talk. What got her was the admission price that I'd stolen from her purse. If it had been to open up a savings account, maybe I'd have been rewarded. But not for wanting to see, "Dose poor animals, half 'sleep in a cage! You see better in TV, in natur'l, witout all de aggravation an' stink!"

I heard ceramic cymbals in the darkness. Cecilia was setting the table but whatever it was that my mother was concocting, smelt obnoxious. Red wine was evaporating, but there was a worse smell, similar to the sharp odour of goats. Cecilia opened the pantry door and I was drowned in it.

"Come and get your din-din," chuckled Cecilia.

It was not the right time or the right place to be picky. But two real life kidneys in the middle of my plate was going too far.

The bed of mashed potatoes transformed into cotton on which lay the relics of a murder victim's autopsy. A naked woman lay face down on an examining table, with two deep, kidney-shaped holes in her lower back. I already had a hard enough time making incisions into meat, how was I supposed to get my fork prongs and knife's teeth into an organ. I was unprepared. I hadn't attended medical school.

"Oh! De best! De juice! Ah!" My mother rushed back to the kitchen.

"Juice" is a fine euphemism for "blood." I grabbed a kidney with my fingers and panicked when I didn't know what to do next.

"I'm going to tell!" warned Cecilia, "You better put it in your mouth right now."

"Please, Cecilia! I'll do anything!" I pleaded with her, my hands cupped in prayer, the kidney somewhere in between.

Nevertheless, she blurted, "Mommy!!"

"The record," I reminded her in a ventriloquist whisper as my mother returned with the saucer and miniature ladle.

"You. Wha' you wan', you big mouth?" my mother covered her ears.

I never understood. My mother's own mouth was nearer to her ears, yet it never hurt them when she was the one who did the screaming.

"Um, some salt, please . . ." muttered Cecilia.

"You don' need no salt! Dere's salt enough in natur'l Mot'her Nature! Don' start now, you, too! Eat!"

I held the kidney under the table while I continued to fork the mashed potatoes into my mouth.

"Kate. I don' wan' see de cherry . . ."

I switched the mashed potatoes to my other cheek. As though I were scratching my neck, I dropped the kidney down the front of my dress. It remained caught in between the fabric and my chest, exactly in the middle like the birth of a unicorn breast.

Cecilia shot me a worried glance. I leaned over my plate so the slackening in the fabric would help it to descend.

"No elbows on de table! How many times mus' I repeat myse'f?"

I straightened. The kidney landed on top of my skinny thighs. Getting up would pose a problem. The kidney would plop down on my mother's plush cream carpet, and God knows what she would think. I pinched the fabric until I managed to get it in my underwear. The feeling of a greasy kidney against my bare skin was revolting. I balanced the second kidney on my fork, nothing in the world could get me to stab it, and brought it to my lips.

Looking at Cecilia, I mouthed, "Moussorgsky."

I lowered it into the collar of my dress while my mother was "cleaning the serving platter," that is, scraping the last crusty, oily bits and licking the spoon. She avoided eye contact with us whenever she did this, embarrassed about her table manners and, even worse, her broken diet. I stretched out the elastic waistband of my white Tuesday underwear, and the kidney fell inside.

After dinner, my mother armed herself for her nightly walk around the block with a towel to swat mosquitoes with, and an orange fluorescent flag to prevent hit-and-runs. She never gave a second's thought to the latter until she heard a talk show about it and now it was a central preoccupation in her life, along with cholesterol, getting struck by lightning and holding your back straight when you picked up a box.

I walked along the sea wall. One kidney fell quickly but the other stubbornly dangled from my underwear. I jumped up and down like a silly little kid.

"Mommy! Look what I can do!"

Faking a tap dance, I pushed both kidneys off the edge with my foot. My new sandals were too big and flopped down noisily. My mother chose sizes that would fit the next year.

"You be careful of de all'gators! You!"

The kidneys floated and oil rainbows sprouted around them in larger and larger circles. The catfish darted up to fight over the remains. I was alarmed to see such a commotion with my mother so near, breaking a basilica leaf and admiring its fragrance, or her ingenuity at having planted the seeds.

"You wan' go for a lil' walk, honey?" she asked.

"I do!" Cecilia slammed the screen porch door, panted down the stepping-stones as though she feared we would leave without her and never come back.

My mother held my right hand and Cecilia's left one down the hot, barren streets of Wachovi. I had to wave the orange flag.

CHAPTER 6

"A'kay . . . yes, a'kay . . ."

My mother twisted the cord of her telephone around her finger. It was an imitation turn of the century model that only the rich would have had back in the days when operators listened in on people's conversations, that she'd purchased for fifty books of green stamps.

"Wunderful . . ."

She sat on the edge of her king-sized bed, looking at a cleanly-shaven leg, front view, side view, and, with an effort, back view.

"Jus' wunderful."

From what I could gather, Ursula was going on a three day Caribbean cruise with Harry. I rolled my mother's panty hose into tight wads and bounced them into the bottom drawer of her dressing table.

"See if you can help me match these," I asked Cecilia.

After folding the towels, sheets, and O.L. handkerchiefs, we were faced with the bottom of the laundry basket, the part we hated most, my mother's knee-highs, which were like amputated stockings. If we got the tint wrong when pairing them, she stuck them in our face to make sure we weren't blind. Cecilia opened the curtains.

"Oh, I don' know 'bout dat. Guard, Ursula, you take me by su'prise . . ." she cuddled the receiver to her breast, "Give time for you eyes to a'just. De air-conditionin's on."

Daylight equalled heat, heat increased electric bills. Cecilia closed the curtains. We were condemned to live in semi-darkness.

"One, bu' only one weeken'. You lil' stinker, you."

The phone cord, wrapped around her wrist was robbing her hand of colour.

"Tommy an' Timmy are comin', so it's not nec'ry to vacuum. I hope dey do not destroy my house." The thought of fingerprints on the refrigerator doors was already ruining her day.

"You. Get dress."

She didn't expand the order to Cecilia, maybe because her one-piece bathing suit had fringes around the bottom like a skirt.

"Can I put on a towel?" I asked, meaning to wrap a beach towel round my hips, Hawaiian-style.

"N. O."

"But you always let me wear it like that?"

"You gettin' tall now, dat don' look good anymore."

I was puzzled. Usually my mother said not to "hoot" about the way we looked.

"It's only Tommy and Timmy, why should I care?"

"You pu' on dis B'yumuda short an' you do no' argue wit' me for once you life."

I sat on my bed, staring down angrily at an ugly pair of army green Bermuda shorts she'd literally found at Gables Beach, in the sand, and now for some reason was making me wear.

"I'm not going to wear something a total stranger wore!" I bawled as my mother passed by my open bedroom door, feeling more sensitive than usual at her accumulated injustices.

"Dey belong-ged to a child. Look, child shorts, wha's de matter wit' you brains?"

"Yuck," Cecilia for once took my side, picking up the pair of shorts by its zipper and dropping them back down with distaste.

"You chil'ren, you sick. Wha' goes on in dere?"

She gave the side of her head little taps then fingered her hair back into place. Her hair reverted back to the eight original curls of her sponge rollers, no matter how often she manipulated it.

"You don't even know if they belonged to a girl or boy," Cecilia argued.

"If the individual did not wear underwear?" I looked as scientifically arrogant as a sob would permit, "Would that not promote leprosy?"

"My Guard, I don' know wha' dis world is comin' to!" my mother stormed out of our room with the shorts.

I felt an impulse to yell something like, "Leprosy!" but I heard the cycle knob of the washing machine being violently turned as she missed the right programme each time.

"Kate?"

My mother could sense a mile away I had opened a book. I liked reading more than anything else and Stag Head was a great listener.

"Kate! I am goin' to count three!"

She made me serve her water on demand, even if the pitcher was less than an arm's length away and I, at the other side of the house. Domestic assistance was one of the reasons I think my mother decided to have children.

"One!"

I pushed through the lines, condemned to the staccato reading which results from loss of concentration.

"TWO!!"

From the tone of my mother's voice, I knew it was something serious like a night-light I'd not turned off or a tap I'd left dripping.

I reached my mother's view by rhythmical, "Three!" though she remained silent. She lay upon a lawn chair, on the dock, under the kumquat tree, wearing above the bellybutton underwear and a cross your heart bra with the familiar ball of tissue paper to absorb the beads of sweat which liked to form in her cleavage. The beads of sweat on her upper lip were disturbing her less. She thought her neighbours from across the canal were too near-sighted to know the difference between underwear and a white bikini. Her legs had razor stubble and baby oil below the knee, and the end of her curled up toes had small bits of skin missing. With a fingernail scissors, she liked to chop off all of the skin she called "dead".

I glanced at the canal, afraid she'd seen the deposit of O-bones and T-bones that the catfish were leaving close to the dock. My mother enjoyed making me stand there and wait as she pretended not to take notice of me.

"You babushka, Kate, how you are wiping it?" she finally spoke.

Heat expanded to my ears. Flabbergasted, I sought the correct response when "fine" came, on its own, to my mouth.

My mother expected geometrical wonders from us. From each square of toilet paper, we were supposed to obtain a series of octagonal wipes.

"You so ce'tain?"

"Yes," I answered though her stare was making me less and less so.

"You star' you days?"

"What days?"

I was too young to know what on earth she could possibly mean.

"A'kay. Follow me."

She allowed me to enter her bathroom after I'd removed my sandals and checked the bottom of both my feet.

"Now, you young, but some girls, dey start, you know, even a' nine, ten, at el'ven. Me, I star' when I was thi'teen. It's a waste, such a shame, Mot'her Nature! A'ready you so skinny, jus' skin an' bones . . ."

"Is something wrong with me?" I squeaked.

"I show you sometin'. Now don' get upset. It is norm'l. I . . . well . . . open you eyes."

Her waste basket wore a thick coat of varnish and shells. My mother pushed aside the loose carpet of short blonde hairs and dirty cotton swabs, until she found what she was looking for. It was wrapped in layers of white toilet paper which she proceeded to unravel like a mummy. Until then, I was almost having fun. Underneath the layers of toilet paper was a tight wad of cotton padding; without a further word of warning, she expanded it.

I don't know what I did first, gasp, shriek, or lift both hands to my forehead. The cotton padding was drenched with blood, vivid shiny red in the middle, like raw flesh; around the contours, it was exactly the brown of a well-done steak.

"Dis was Mótina's." She ignored my agitation.

"You cut yourself again shaving?"

I pressed my stomach, my face, my watery eyes. The women of my mother's single blade razor generation always had, I noticed, regularly chipped white scars down their shin bones. I imagined my mother shaving the skin off her shin, tan on the outside, white on the inside, like a potato peeling.

"Now, dis happens to ev'ry woman, we lose a lil' blood, ev'ry month. Dis is wha' makes us a woman. Even if you a child still in you mind, you body is 'coming a woman."

"A little?! Oh my God, no! From where? My babushka??"

She answered quietly, "No. You lil' sis'er."

I instinctively knew she was not referring to Cecilia. A wave of outrage swelled in me.

"I'll urinate blood?!"

The toilet bowl filled with tomato soup; macaroni hands, feet, buttocks, breasts floated to the steamy top . . . Harry lapped Ursula's mess like a dog.

I sunk to my knees. If I had had the strength, I would have crawled to the sink and held my wrists under the water. I was victim to one of those preliminary heaves of vomit.

"Now don' get all upset wit' Mot'her Nature."

"Why do we have to urinate blood??"

"Honey. You don' urnate. It's jus' a fact o' life."

I could tell she was holding back. Probably the sucking out part, like when a scorpion stings a victim and an Indian has to suck the poison out of the wound and spit. I saw that once on Bonanza, I think.

"Just like that?"

"From dere, you make you poo-poo."

"I know that!"

"From dis, you make urina. Well, dere, b'tween."

I bent forward as much as I could.

"You see?"

"No."

In a state of shock, I stared instead at the pendant necklace she was wearing. The multi-carat ruby shone like a sanguine sun. It used to be on the ring my father gave her at Niagara Falls when he popped the question, which she readily accepted upon seeing the stone.

"Well, dere is a hole dere. It still too lil', but it will get more big later!" she stunned me out of my stupor.

"Why?"

"Why we have hairs? Why we have a nose? It's like dat. You accept!"

I was offered an elastic belt with metal hooks onto which I could attach a wad of cotton padding. Securing it in place was the same principle as stabbing a hook into bait. It was big enough for a Red Cross nurse to dress a wounded soldier.

"But how will I know when it will open?"

"You did no' feel any ting?!"

"I didn't start bleeding yet."

"Yes you did. You don' feel?!"

I remained wordless, thoughtless.

"You don' see?!" her tone rose, "Me, I see!"

Though my mother was shorter than me, her stride was longer, and her steps, more rapid. In the utility room, she confronted me with my Tuesday, and four pairs of my Friday underwear. When she fought for these in the clearance sale bins, she was more concerned with the colour white than the days of the week. Each bore a meat stain from what I'd hidden down there. I underwent the humiliation of her sticking a pair in my face. Although to my mother all her neighbours were near-sighted, her own offspring were far-sighted. I had been careful to hide the underwear in the middle of the laundry basket, but my mother washed even the whites in cold water to save electricity and traces of brown had remained. My forearms lifted to protect my guilt-laden face.

"It's a'kay, honey. It's no' yo' fault," she reassured me, "De world mus' turn."

CHAPTER 7

The three of us waited outside for the Tattas to arrive, hostesses of a solemn reception. Most of our neighbours simply let their guests in and out the front door without formality. We always had to help ours in and out of their car doors. This must have been some old Eastern European tradition, dating back to the horse and carriage when the beloved one needed a hand to make it down the high step; or dating back to the invention of the first car, when the entire village wouldn't miss its arrival or departure for the world.

Ursula and Harry's light blue Lincoln Continental turned lazily into our driveway, the wheels making crackling noises over the residues of sand. I stood awkwardly, looking at my own reflection in the tinted window instead of opening the door. How thin I looked, and dark beneath the eyes. The electric window descended, swallowing me and simultaneously giving birth to Harry's bald head and white suit. The air coming out of their car was a mixed blessing, wonderfully cold yet saturated with stale cigarette smoke and aftershave.

"Hi there, baby doll," Harry greeted me with amused eyes and a wink, absentmindedly inaugurating his emergency brake.

"Cut it out, Harry!" Ursula shot Harry a discontented glance and squeezed his knee. There were white marks around her fingers where she'd removed her rings.

"Don' run in my driveway! You get black oil on you feet, you drag all 'cross my house!" my mother warned Tommy and Timmy, "I do not wan'. Be care, my cactus!"

"Boys will be boys," laughed Harry and handed my mother the red suitcase Ursula had brought over last time, and a shopping bag full of sandy flip-flops and a greasy tube of sun block without a cap.

"My guard, my guard, wha' I get myself talk-ked into!" my mother joked, but there was something sad and weary in her eyes, usually sharp and accusing, that made me go and put my arm around her shoulders protectively. Melancholic people can go through life with bloodhound eyes, they receive little compassion, but bad-tempered people need only look discouraged one minute, and they get whatever they want. Ursula and Harry waved to us as they pulled out of the driveway. I rested my chin affectionately on her head. "Aya! Don' do dat. You stringbean! You hurt my neck!" was the thanks I got.

"Now you stay outside an' play! I don' wan' no one in my house, in an' out, wit you dirty feet!"

The others ran down to the canal. I staggered slowly after them. I didn't feel like a child any more. I felt that the revelation my mother had made to me, of losing for some unknown reason quantities of my own blood and having to dress the wound all by myself made playing impossible. I foresaw a dismal life in that mature weirdness where play was undesirable to every adult.

Cecilia watched with amazement as Timmy and Tommy pulled up the dripping crab trap. They found a host of pig tails inside, caught here and there among the rusty grilles like waterlogged carrots. A stench rose, similar to the fish that float down the canal, swollen and upside down. Along the bottom of the trap, scrambled the multitude of armoured legs belonging to a forlorn navy of stone crabs. They faced us heroically, each holding out a single overgrown pincer.

Timmy forced a kumquat branch into the trap. When he tilted it, three crabs hung on stubbornly.

"Stop it! I'm going to tell! That one's just a baby!" The tension in me sought release.

"That one's just a baby!" Tommy Tatta imitated me.

"It doesn't really matter, Kate. Mommy says we're having them for dinner on Sunday."

Tommy let out a violent, "Ugh! Better not be with prunes!"

The trap splashed back into the canal, the brownish water lifting the crabs just enough to give them hope before they were plunged to the murky bottom again.

Tommy, tired of swimming, knocked on the screen of our patio. He didn't know that if it loosened, he would be subject to the medieval kind of punishment one still found within my mother's realm.

"You aren't allowed to go in anyway when you're wet."

"I gotta! Tell your mom to open up."

"Just go behind a tree. Don't make a big deal about it," I advised him for his own sake as well as mine.

"I don't want everyone to see."

"See what?" I pried.

"My Oscar Meyer weenie."

I thought his answer oddly corresponded to my absurdest whims and puzzled over it, with ketchup, mustard and relish. I was more convinced than ever that whatever it was, it was edible. For some unknown reason, I began to resent him. Maybe it was the hint of arrogance in his words, "My Oscar Meyer weenie," insinuating whatever he had, I did not.

Timmy and Cecilia bent down under the dock to discern spitting barnacles and hermit crabs. The tide was high and they waved their fingertips around in figures of eight. There Tommy was standing, his back to me, with his bathing suit bottom still on, yet a long yellow arch of urine swayed left and right as though he were watering flowers with a garden hose.

"Where are you, Kate?" I should have known I could count on my sister to jeopardize my position.

Tommy turned slightly, and I saw he was definitely holding something in his hand; it was a cross between a gigantic earthworm and a small bratwurst. It had a tiny mouth and no eyes whatsoever.

"Kate?!" she called again with such insistence, as though

my seeing whatever crustacean she had found were a matter of life or death.

The underdeveloped creature wriggled in dissent before Tommy hid it. I saw it thrash to the left and right. It was the embryo of a fire-spitting dragon. Just as a grape-sized egg yields forth a crocodile, it, too, would grow up into something horrendous.

A leech suckled my monthly blood until it grew teeth with which it began to gnaw a tunnel inside me. It grew scales, claws and a single horn, tools it used to scrape its way further into my flesh.

I read to Stag Head, "That is why a man will leave his father and his mother and he must *cleave* to his wife and they must become one flesh . . . " "I will greatly multiply your pain in childbearing, in pain you shall bring forth children, yet your desire shall be for your husband."

So I would hunger for my husband's flesh, and he would crave for mine. I closed the Bible. Conspiracy was in the air, I could smell it like the unseen smoke of a distant barbecue. Parents hid the gruesome facts of life from their children. No wonder they always had to be alone to converse freely.

CHAPTER 8

Our boat hung on davits so it wouldn't become home to a colony of barnacles. I lay on its deck, listening to the canal, the lapping of the sea walls, the occasional gulps under the dock, the thumps and rubbery screeches of other boats colliding into the tyres thrown over the half-waterlogged, half-scorched poles of their docks.

I smelt lighter fluid on the breath of the hot breeze hitting my face. I stared into the setting sun until I could project small suns wherever I looked. The Minsky family had arrived and Joseph was pulling in the cord of the crab trap. The first few feet were white followed by the slimy green part of the cord that usually remained beneath the waterline. That's when whoever did the pulling was less enthusiastic.

With tongs, Joseph grabbed the first stone crab by the big claw. The second crab hooked itself onto the bottom of the trap, and he was pulling it up, upside down, by a back leg. I projected a sanguine spot onto the back of his dark curly hair, and bang, shot him. Sharon held a bucket near to the trap so Joseph could knock the third obstinately clinging crab off the grille and into it.

"De children? Where dey dis'pear?!" my mother asked, with regal offence.

As long as the three of them were having martinis, she hadn't really cared but now it was time for dinner to be served.

"Oh, they're taking a look at the new house, they're not doing any harm," answered Sharon.

A new house in Florida means one in mid-construction. It is common practice for neighbours to tour these whenever there aren't any workers around, count the number of bedrooms and bathrooms, calculate the ratio. People generally know which state up north the owners will come from, but nothing more about them besides the real estate agency that made the sale. During the two to three odd months it takes to build the new house, the future inhabitants are subject to debate. Anyone having a chimney or a high dome ceiling installed is made fun of and probably will never fit in. A built-in bar makes potential friends. A sunken living room is taboo, since most Wachovi citizens are past their prime. After a few drinks, their hips break easily. When the owners finally move in, and shortly thereafter offer their new neighbours a tour of their house, they do not realize that the oohing and aahing imposters know their house better than they do, and were the first to use their loo.

My mother commenced the tour of her lawn. Whether Sharon and Joseph wanted it or not, they were about to get a review of every plant, tree, bud and sprout. The avocado tree, as by now everyone alive must have known, started as a pip a few years back. My mother had stuck toothpicks in it, submerged it in a cup of water and roots had sprung. The resulting lanky tree, heavy with free avocadoes, was once a brown orb, no bigger than a golf ball.

"You do de crabs, now, de barbecue, it's a'kay," ordered my mother as soon as she noticed me jump off the boat and land on my hands and knees on the gravel.

She was about to show Sharon and Joseph her pride and joy, a three inch high banyan tree, plucked from the famous original at the Edison Winter Home. My mother thought one day it would give her shade and liked the idea of its roots being long enough to drink from Mr. Walter's yard instead of hers.

"Why me?" I appealed.

"B'cause already I slave all day. You, where you dis'pear all day, you?"

Sharon and Joseph could not stop themselves from smiling. Actually, Joseph had lit the barbecue, fetched the crabs and made the martinis. Sharon had brought over the potato salad, the devilled eggs and the dessert, the only sure way to have gotten any around our place, other than dried fruit. And I had set the table, which on top of my daily chores, exceeded by far hers, namely shaving her legs and painting her toenails coral pink.

"I mean, I don't know how," I argued, not wanting to know, either.

"Look! It so easy!" my mother hammered, "You jus' take an' . . ."

She lifted a crab up by its weaker claw and in her impatience, broke it off while thrusting it onto its back on the red-hot grill. The six hairy legs jerked spasmodically, somewhat like an overturned beetle propels its legs against thin air.

The flames rose up around the crab. With its remaining claw, it struggled to grab onto something to pull itself away from the pain and managed to take hold of my mother's tongs. The jointed legs agitated in a frenzy to escape when my mother squeezed the tongs this time tightly across the armoured torso, holding it securely in place over the highest flame, until the creature started to scream. I didn't know crabs had voices. Though not loud, the cry was pathetic and shrill and sent a shiver through me.

"You see?" my mother casually asked before leaving me there with the rest of the bucket's contents.

This one was already undergoing the transformation from life to food. Only a last leg slowly jerked its goodbye.

With the tongs, I peered into the bucket. I felt like a giant crab myself, about to pinch the next victim. The crabs' mouths were vertical, champing nothing and spitting water like a suite of tiny panels. Their tiny eyes were propped up and leaned back and forth, begging for mercy. That was it. I grabbed hold of the plastic bucket, ran panting down to the canal and threw them back in.

"How you gettin' 'long, Kate?" my mother inquired from the air-conditioning compressor.

The tour was coming to an end as she showed her latest aloe plant that looked like a cross between a cactus and octopus tentacle. If one broke the tip off, the extracts were said to be beneficial for healing burns. The other children had returned and were standing around me, sunburnt and mosquito bitten.

"Go and wash your hands," Sharon ordered the children.

My mother intercepted them.

"You don' need to go 'cross de whole house. Dip in de swimmin' pool! Jus' dip, dat's 'nough."

Everyone was sitting around the picnic table of our patio when I brought the silver dome on a platter. My mother straightened her back and lifted her chin an inch; she presided at the head of the table; on backless bench to her right, sat Joseph, Sharon, Rosa and Lucy Minsky; on the bench to her left, Tommy and Timmy Tatta, Cecilia, and the empty space for me. Tommy was busy mashing his baked potato and Timmy was picking the skin of a broken sun blister off his shoulder. Sharon and Joseph smiled at me so sweetly, that it was like a magnetic force that made the corners of my mouth yield upwards, too.

"What is it?" asked Lucy.

"Not the Easter bunny again, I hope," I heard Rosa whisper under Sharon's loud, "Shh!"

Sharon opened her paper napkin which my mother had cut in two; it fell apart into two squares so thin, the ceiling fan, even at the lowest speed, forced her to cross her legs to hold them in place.

"Wha' you waitin' for?!"

When my mother's juices began to flow, she could become aggressive. I should have crawled under my bed, but instead I lifted the dome. One burnt stone crab lay on its back upon the silver platter.

"Where are de ot'hers?!"

"Home . . . " was all I managed to pronounce. I hadn't a drop of saliva left in my mouth.

"You! Where, home?! De kitchen?" She stood up. "Do you hear me?!"

If I did, I couldn't any more because I had just received a smack on my ear hard enough to make it ring. Lucy and Rosa lowered their heads on the table and began to cry, not because there was nothing to eat, but because I had been hit. Cecilia used to cry, too, but she was used to it by now. Their sobs gave me courage and I found myself screaming at the top of my voice, "Home in the canal!" several times on end.

This somehow calmed my mother who sat back down and let her arms hang limply off her lawn chair, as though her jewelry had really been stolen, for once. Sharon hadn't spoken yet but looked back and forth as though she were watching a table tennis match with equal sympathy for both Chinese players. Joseph kept his eyes down on his baked potato, and poked holes in the aluminum paper.

"It doesn't matter, Olga, ah, poor thing, I know how she feels, the little darling . . ."

I could tell Sharon's words had no effect whatsoever in softening my mother. Human kindness to her was equivalent to stupidity. When volunteers came to the door to collect, my mother was already in mid-calculation: she took a walk around the block anyway, so if she could earn a few dollars a night in doing so . . . It is very painful for me to admit that my mother helped herself to the handsomest bills in the American Cancer Society and Multiple Sclerosis cans she toted around. Some community members put their bills in envelopes. These were opened with the steam of a consommé de homard or beef broth, one dollar put in their place, and closed. My mother said the organizations were crooks and only ten percent made it to the sick or handicapped. Like the food chain, she felt somewhere along the line, she deserved her piece of the pie.

"Should I order a pizza?" Joseph asked.

The "yeahs" of youth were forceful, though I dared not join in. I looked down at the pebble-stone floor, which even in the worst of circumstances reminded me of some sticky treat.

"Such beaut'ful crab an' we are goin' to eat ar'ficial, man-made pizza!" "Man-made", was the worst insult my mother could verbalize. With it, I received a series of pinches on my neck, face, stomach and thighs, hard enough to make me scream. There was no flotilla of crabs around to defend me. That's when Lucy sought refuge in her father's frail, fair arms and begged to be taken back home.

Cecilia's chin dimpled, which it always did when she tried not to cry.

"No!" protested Rosa, "If we go, she'll kill her!"

Her father apparently agreed, for he proposed to take all of us out to the Red Lobster, where my mother could taste the "Loving Couple", a thick, juicy filet mignon snuggling up to a lobster tail. His description was persuasive. To my relief, my mother accepted the invitation. I knew I would not be allowed to go, yet sensed that standing by Sharon and Joseph Minsky's van before my mother ordered me into the pantry closet would reduce my sentence, especially if I wailed audibly on my way in.

Really, I didn't care as much as they thought. I wasn't hungry, for I'd swallowed enough of my snot and tears. Pantry closet time in my mother's absence was based on the honour system, as though she had given us the right example in valuing such things. I went to the pantry closet for a stepladder, and brought Stag Head down from the wall. I placed him on the glass table, balancing him on his wooden plaque.

At first, Stag Head was unused to a vertical position, and even nauseous, which I suppose after so many years of looking only straight ahead across our dining room, should be expected, though this did strike me as odd for he no longer had a stomach. I put his plaque against my face and gave him a run across the house, imagining my father was chasing us with a gun. It was great fun.

Out of breath, I squatted down and held Stag Head's neck between my knobbly knees. I stroked the hairs on his head and neck, at least down to where it had been severed. I cupped my hands over the plastic bulbs someone had exchanged for his eyes, lifting them as though they were his own eyelids. The spirit of life regained him, as did his affection for me.

When Stag Head recovered his place on the unchanging wall, I entered the closet and closed the door. Only in the darkness, can one hear one's own breathing. Only in darkness, does one strain the eyes for light. I did, until the darkness moved, like a thousand flies. Closing my lids and opening them made no difference. Blackness lives, dances, too, like anyone knows who has long observed it.

CHAPTER 9

"Mamà! Mótina! Mótina! Stop! Can we *please* have a Christmas tree?!" begged Cecilia, tapping my mother's knee insistently as though this would make the car stop.

"You a'ready had one in de school. How many you need?"

Cecilia needed a pair of blunt scissors with which to make four-leaf clover looking snowflakes and that was about how much our mother was going to invest in anyone's commercialized American Christmas for that year.

"One for at home just once in our lives! *Please!*"

"You a'ready had one, you don' remember?"

My mother kept a mental list of all that was already done once in anyone's lifetime. Repetition to her was superfluous; it was even more abominable; it was a waste.

"No!" wailed Cecilia, who never lied.

Cecilia had been too young. I still remembered our mother in her shaggy fur coat, Cecilia and I used to pretend we were brown bears in it, and an axe, chopping down a pine tree in New Hampshire and dragging it back to the car on the outskirts of a highway. Its tip swished in the snow like a dragon tail. I distinctly recall this detail because I was worried that the trail would scare away the forest fighters. I was commissioned to walk ahead, and warn them if I saw anybody coming, because the forest, our mother warned us, was full of criminals.

"Well, me, I remember. De needles, dey fall an' make a mess. Dey block my vacuum cleaner, de sac is a'ways full. De wood, wha' we do wit' it after? We have no chimney in Flor'da!" What she seemed to be getting at was, "No."

Cecilia sobbed, stating that we never got to have anything. For a split second, I saw my mother's eyes in the rear-view mirror guiltily staring ahead, and not quite at the road. She took Cecilia more seriously than she did me. Cecilia was easier to please.

As soon as we got home, my mother slid open the linen closet and stamped her foot.

"Here! An' don' bother me no more!"

She tossed Cecilia and I a Christmas tree about eight inches high. It was actually a napkin-holder someone at church had given to her, that she had been saving as a gift for someone else. It was composed of two side by side flat wooden Christmas trees, painted picnic table green. The inside, where napkins were supposed to stand, was bare unvarnished pine wood, with visible knots to vouch for the once outstretched branches. Cecilia beamed with joy.

"You. Wha' you say?" my mother threatened me.

I was regularly starting to have what she called, "dat look o'er my face".

"Thank you very much, Mommy," I recited, feeling the look accentuating.

Cecilia and I hesitated where to place it. The dinner table elevated our tree to an appropriate height, but on it, it really looked like a napkin-holder. My mother's record player was out of the question, it might scratch. The floor was problematic; it accentuated the puny size, and gave one the impression the napkin-holder had fallen off the table. Anyone walking by would pick it up and put it back on the table. I finally suggested "Fool's Stool", which I sensed I had outgrown. Cecilia positioned our Christmas tree on top of it. I wound my bathrobe around the base. I knew no needles would fall, but it made the composition look fuller. My mother took a picture.

We didn't have a manger, but annually, our mother let us have things from the kitchen to make one. Jesus, like every year, was an almond wrapped in exactly one square of pink toilet paper. Mary was the whitish, bottom part of a stick of celery, the only thing we could find that looked like a flowing gown. Joseph was a small carrot. Three cauliflower heads were the sheep. That was all we were allowed to have, besides a cutting board on which to arrange them. Cecilia requested some broccoli for the landscape, but my mother dryly replied that there were no trees in Jerusalem.

Jesus was all that had survived by midnight mass. Mary, Joseph and the three sheep were sliced into a Caesar's salad when they had begun to wilt. At first I screamed, but my mother assured me this would not hurt their resurrection. As I ate them, I wondered if things eaten by me would resurrect with me, as part of me, or if eaten things would resurrect directly out of me,

I rubbed my eyes sleepily. The church bell, a recent donation of the Knights of Columbus, tolled midnight. Cecilia was sound asleep at my mother's side, despite the organ that seemed to pump a strange, spiritual life into St. Andrew's cement vaulted veins. In a corner, a statue of the Virgin Mary offered her breast to Jesus, a happy, healthy baby. Jesus as an adult was unrecognizable; He was sickly looking, emaciated, unhappy; I felt weak looking at Him as He bled and bled on the cross. Mankind must stop sinning or Jesus would soon be eaten away. As it was, His ribs had nearly broken out of the skin of His torso; there were more tendons on His arms and legs than meat; His feet were so bony, one could discern every detail of their skeletal structure; and yet the blood continued to drip, and mankind continued to eat Him, though anyone would have to admit, He was far from appetizing.

The priest's voice roused the congregation. In oneness, it stood and was seated, bowed and lifted its head, sang Hallelujah and Hosanna, breathed Amen. Only an occasional cough or infectious snort broke the charm, reminding us we still had our feet on the earth.

The priest preached, "See, the Lamb of God that takes away the sin of the world."

To my dismay, an image invaded my mind, an horrific image of Jesus, lamb, roasting upon a rotating cross. The lamb's skin was evenly crispy; juice and melted fat fell freely from the small, pitiful body . . . I closed my eyes to make it disappear.

The priest preached, "Keep your senses, be watchful. Your adversary, the Devil, walks about like a roaring lion, seeking to devour someone."

I knew it was time to eat Jesus, for the baskets were being passed down the rows. Mass was more like a self-service cafeteria where one pays then eats, than a restaurant where one eats then pays. My mother put in a nickel for me, and a dime for her. She wasn't about to pay for Cecilia, who was sleeping. My mother, I noticed, was always friendlier with her neighbours before the Eucharist, when they would shake her hand and say, "Peace be with you," than when they passed her the basket.

The priest held a wafer out to me: "The body of Christ."

I saw myself as a composite creature of the Middle Ages. My mouth was open like a young bird's, my tongue flat as a cow's, and my teeth as buck as a rabbit's. As the wafer laid on my tongue, I tried not to think that Christ's entire body was in my mouth, compressed to a bite-size portion for my own salvation.

With my tongue, I tried moving Him from left to right but He stuck to the roof of my mouth and though I knew it was bad manners, I had to use a finger to get Him down. However I attempted to encourage myself, I could not bring myself to chew Him. My saliva rose and eventually softened Him, until He was like a tiny mouthful of dough, which I swallowed. If I am completely honest, I must admit that I was glad to be rid of Him; He was far from the most delectable thing I'd been forced to eat. I concentrated on my body to see if I felt a difference now that He was in me, becoming an integral part of me. I know this will sound strange, but it felt as if the dough began to rise, to expand until He filled me, stretched me out. My skin tingled everywhere and I was filled with a sensation of well-being I had never known before. Organ music and voices of all ages mixed. Christ was in me. I could feel Him, it was like love growing. It was rapture.

A bit of stray Eucharist found itself trapped within the crevice of my molar. With my tongue, I nudged it out, wondering if it weren't by chance the finger or some other small leftover from Our Saviour, when an amazing thing happened. Where for so many years the idea of eating flesh had accumulated into a mountain of revulsion, this last thought suddenly pushed my revulsion to such an extreme that it was like toiling up one side of the mountain before tumbling down the other side. I was unprepared. I had only seen the first half of the mountain I thought went eternally up.

Something new was opening up in me, a strange new appetite from somewhere below, a pleasant tug which I wished to satisfy, and then again, did not.

I squeezed my knees together like Jesus did on the cross. I wanted to hold my arms out wide open and hug anyone or anything, even a pillar. The Holy Spirit, I thought, was flooding me with love, a love so great I could have eaten any of my neighbours. My heart thumped wildly at this thought, as I stared at the strong veined hand of a man in the pew in front of me. In my mind, I nibbled at the webbed skin between his strong fingers. My body tensed with an ever growing hunger.

A woman was holding a baby so chunky that its arm was dimpled where there should have been an elbow. Each time the baby began to cry, the woman simulated eating it. I wanted to groan, scream, tell everyone I loved them, and would gladly eat them. I imagined the fattest women in the church, Belinda Moors, naked on all fours as her doughy breasts dragged on the floor. I imagined kneading them with my hands and face, tugging at them with my teeth.

That thought was the drop that made the bowl spill over. I gasped loudly, clutching at my stomach as my whole body underwent a series of contractions. Those in my vicinity, including my own mother, looked at me alarmed, as though I were going to be sick. The woman with the baby offered me a putridly sweet smelling rag.

"You. Wha's de matter wit' you?!" my mother asked me as we left mass.

For some reason, I felt horrendously ashamed. Pleasure seemed more embarrassing to confess than did pain.

"It felt like someone kept stabbing a knife into me, here," I misled her as I pressed down on my lower stomach.

Belinda Moors smiled at me before getting into her old dented beetle. I turned my head the other way. The blood that had invaded my lower parts rose to heat my face with shame.

I helped my mother carry Cecilia back to bed. As soon as the lights in the house went out, I slipped into our bathroom. I expected, anxiously wrenching my underwear down to my knees, to find blood, or some side effect of the newly opened hole. All the way home, I'd sensed my crotch was drenched. I was bewildered to find nothing of the sort, let alone a colourful drop.

Upon closer examination, I discovered a gooey substance, that of egg white, that had miraculously dripped out of my flesh and onto my underwear. I pinched some off the fabric, though it was not at all easy to seize. As I slowly opened my first three fingers like an orchid come to life, I studied the tightrope lines it left in between, like when someone sleeping yawns and a similar gooeyness trails between their upper and lower teeth. If beaten, would it make a meringue, I wondered, at the same time fascinated by and disgusted at Mother Nature's recycling ability.

CHAPTER 10

"Are you sure, Mrs. Lester, she's menstruating?"

Dr. Kreushkin fingered my boobies; I kicked my legs and shrieked with laughter.

"Wha' you mean, am I sure? She ruined me a whole week of un'erwears, de child, den it stop like dat, for months, an' now she has pains like a knife in her ovries . . ."

"What are ovries?" I sat up on the examining table to ask; the long paper towel doctors cover their examining tables with fell off the side.

"You, please keep quite, you."

"When you say she bled, did she flow heavily or just spot?"

"Spot, only spot, bu' she so skinny, look a' her, how can you expect more?"

My mother used her hands to brush my hair away from my face as she spoke, gathered it together like a ponytail, and looked around for an elastic band; finding none, she held it there too tightly.

Dr. Kreushkin contemplated my young body that my baggy white Tuesday underwear and bare feet only accentuated; it looked like I was wearing a nappy. When Dr. Kreushkin asked me to take my underwear off, I stared at the wall, and wished I could be sucked into it. I untangled the undies from my feet, glanced worriedly at my crotch, and looked around as to where I could dispose of them, when my mother offered me her hand.

Dr. Kreushkin opened my legs and then bent each one. He slid his hands into a pair of disposable dishwashing gloves. Before he even touched me, I closed my legs tightly.

"Come, come, I'm not going to bite . . ."

Denying it meant the idea was going through his mind. If he was searching for the mysterious hole, he wasn't about to find it for I myself had already looked, and with the magnifying side of my mother's dressing table mirror where even a pore looks like a crater, and a face, the last thing in the world anyone would want to walk around and face people with.

"Do I have a right to know what you're searching for? Did I do something wrong? Am I being punished for . . . something I did?"

Dr. Kreushkin's eyes widened in surprise, which exposed the upper pink edges of the lower eyelids that have always reminded me of ham.

"Mrs. Lester? Haven't you taken the time to explain the facts of life to your daughter?"

"I a'ready explain all, she knows ev'ryting dere is to know."

My mother drew my hair together again and began to toy around with it; she hesitated between a ballerina bun, tight and high on top of my head, or a schoolteacher's bun, coming loose at the nape.

"Does she comprehend the function of the ovaries?"

I could tell she was about to say I did and since I would not be allowed to contradict her, I spoke up, "No! What are ovaries?"

She dropped my hair back onto my shoulders, shot me a look of contempt, "Egg! You have egg!! So, nosy, you more hap'pay now to know?!"

No wonder egg white had already started seeping out of me, and my mother had two hollow egg shells on her dresser, with a photo of Cecilia and I each inside.

"How can the baby breathe? Is there air in the egg shell?"

Dr. Kreushkin checked my mother's face and his watch before responding that the egg is more like a seed in a woman's stomach from which a tree grows than an egg from which a baby hatches.

"But how does the baby breathe in there?"

What I really wished to understand was how much air must

be pumped into a woman's stomach and if the hole weren't a sort of valve like one used to inflate a bicycle tyre.

My mother scratched the back of her neck and turned to the side as Dr. Kreushkin explained to me the miracle of life, that because the earth used to be entirely covered with water and we all originated from the sea, a woman's stomach contains water during pregnancy and not air. He was just revealing how an unborn baby at one point develops short-term gills, a residue of evolution, when my mother censored his speech with a shift of her ice-blue eyes in his direction; she handed me back my underwear.

I was overtaken by unexpected bliss. How logical it all suddenly seemed. Noah's ark had sailed the flooded earth, the waters after forty days subsided, and now on land, high and dry, there lingered puddles in a woman's stomach. Newborns's eyes, Mrs. Wella had told us, are always blue, be the infant red, black, yellow or white. Noah's flood has lingered, I thought, in places long forgotten.

As I was getting dressed, I could hear Dr. Kreushkin and my mother talking in the next room about whether it would be better to regulate my bleeding with patience rather than with some substance they simply referred to as "the pill".

"Excuse me," I fumbled to fasten my oversized sandals, "How am I to know when a baby will come out of me?"

My mother's reply was imprecise, like when would I stop growing, or be allowed to listen to music when I wanted to without asking: "De time will come." Such a reply was nonetheless reassuring, because the time had come for me to walk instead of crawl, to have knees clear of scabs, and to be able to sleep without checking under my bed to make sure no one was there; so time, though slow in coming, comes.

Dr. Kreushkin's reply was vaguer than my mother's, it hid the truth in just another cabbage patch: "The egg must be fertilized first, Kate, in order to grow . . ."

My mother opened the door and held her hand out to me.

Dr. Kreushkin kept hold of my shoulders, "Kate. You look troubled. Are there specific questions that are bothering you?"

It was now or never. Maybe something was wrong with me, and I should mention it to a doctor. How could I word it? I didn't have the vocabulary for the symptoms.

"Well . . . actually there *is* something that's bothering me . . . down there."

"Where, exactly?"

I don't know how I mastered the courage, but this time I pointed directly at the zone between my legs.

". . . and it . . . itches. It itches. Not a little itch, no, a big big itch that scratching doesn't help. An itch deep inside of me. An itch that wants relief, although in a way, it doesn't."

When I first heard myself use the word "itch", I was disappointed with myself, a hopeless coward; but the more I went on, the more I found the way I put it was actually quite nice.

Dr. Kreushkin looked at my mother calmly. "Yeast infection."

"A' her age? So lil'?"

Yeast? I'd misheard.

"A wet bathing suit, that's all it takes for yeast infection, Mrs. Lester."

"Yeast, as in *bread*?"

"Yes, all women have yeast inside of them, there where it itches you inside, Kate."

"The Bible says a man will leave his father and his mother and he must *cleave* to his wife and they must become one flesh. How do man and wife become one flesh?"

Dr. Kreushkin was going to tell me something, but my mother pleaded, "Don' put any more ideas into de child's brains, please, dat's 'nough for today!"

I changed my tactic.

"How is the egg, hm-hm, 'fertilized?' "

"Look at de child, how she's all excit-ed, she's sweatin', look, her forehead, please, no more."

Dr. Kreushkin lowered his eyes and the side of his mouth twitched; I would never know those words that tried to get out.

CHAPTER 11

"I knew damn well something was going on. I knew it. I could feel it in my bones. He brings the boys over to his mother's, it takes two hours normally, back and forth. No, he comes home again at eleven. Quarter after. I don't say a thing. Just keep watching the news. But inside, I'm boiling up. He thinks he's winning. I'm keeping my big mouth shut. One three day cruise and my mouth's sealed for good. That's what *he* thinks. You're never gonna believe what I did, Olga, you're never gonna believe . . ."

"Cecilia, put sometin' on you head to protect you. I don' wan' de wind to burn you! You hear me?"

Ursula waited for my mother to turn back to her so she could continue her story.

"For hours I listened to him snore away. Nothing could trouble Harry's conscience. I think I could've killed him in his sleep. Finally, I couldn't stand it, I got up, must of been three in the morning. By dawn, I cracked the code of his briefcase. It was both our sons' birthdays, backwards. You had to think of it. I took his keys and made doubles before he was up; he was singing La Bamba in the shower when I came back. I don't think he even noticed I was gone, the s.o.b."

My mother opened the cooler and gave Ursula a plastic cup of wine with pieces of our neighbours' fruits in it. A boat's wake struck us and half of it spilled.

"Monday, I waited in the street two hours 'til his secretary left for lunch. I had to force the key, but it worked; I go in expecting to find all kinds of stuff, you know, pictures of her naked, jewelry bills, that kind of thing. What do I find? Our wedding picture right there on his desk like it always was. After a while, I start wondering if I'm not paranoid. But some voice inside me says, 'Ursula, wait.' So I wait. Then I can't stand it, I'm tired, I'm starving, I go back outside and grab myself a beef-n-chedder at Arby's, and as I'm about to leave, a voice tells me, 'Ursula, go back'."

A tingle went down my spine. Something was nibbling on my bait. The nose of my pole dipped once, violently, and rose. Whatever it was, was gone. The shrimp was on its way to something else. I could feel the hook snagging the seaweed on the bottom as I reeled it back in. My mother contemplated me angrily.

"I couldn't have been gone more than ten, fifteen minutes. The door was unlocked, I walked right in. Olga, you'll never guess what I found, oh my God, Olga . . ."

"Girls, go for a lil' swim for you circulation, it do you good."

"The water's cold, Mótina. I'm fine."

"Yeah, we're fine," Cecilia echoed.

"Do I have to coun' three?"

Cecilia doggy-paddled towards the sand bar. The sand-pipers guessed her intentions and were far up in the air before she'd accomplished two strokes, or rather, splashy slaps. I hung onto the back of the boat.

"There they were, both of them! On the floor on all fours! Like animals! She was wearing an apron, and her dress was up over her big fat ass and Harry was busy smacking it with the sole of his shoe! Can you imagine? The sole of the shoe I gave him two years ago for his birthday!"

The image of a butcher striking a strip of meat with a metal block utensil came to my mind. Was Harry tenderizing the woman's ass? I fell back into the dead man's float.

"Oh my Guard! My Guard!"

"That's not it. I stood there watching. They didn't even see me. The more I looked at the woman, the more I said to myself, 'Come on, Ursula, you know the lady,' but I couldn't quite place her out of context. I thought at first it was one of the boys' teachers, then it dawned on me. You remember

Betty, the baker from Winn Dixie? I'll never buy bread from her again!"

I looked around for Cecilia; she was squatting on the sand bar, poking sea pencils into the wet sand.

"Tsu, tsu, Ursula, calm down, it not worth you healt'. Please."

"I didn't know what the hell I should do! Scream or cry or run. The next thing I knew, I took off my shoe and gave it to Harry! The more I hit him, the more he squeezed her ass and yelled in pain, and the more she thought he was liking it! I was about to shove it up her you know what, but he wrenched it out of my hand. Defending her, when he should have been thinking about me, about my feelings!"

"When you have chil'ren, you don' do such tings! You put de chil'ren first!"

"Harry says I was spying on him. I don't trust him. I ended up having to apologize. I said, quote, 'I am very sorry to have disturbed you and your piece of ass,' unquote. Haven't seen him since. He says if I really loved him, I would understand he needs it. Don't know what he's trying to prove. That he's still got enough juice to go around? She can have it! I'm not going to share any more!"

"Drãmos! Nè, nè! Juokãvo!! Baislùs, baislùs, bjaurlùs!" When my mother depleted her stock of American interjections, she spoke Lithuanian to God in the sky, with her arms as well as her words. Actually, she spoke less than she *hollered, bellowed* in Lithuanian; when she addressed God, she figured her words had a longer way to go.

CHAPTER 12

I set the bowl of shrimp down on the table. Ursula's expression underwent that subtle change when a guest turns into a victim. She recognized what we were about to eat as our former bait. I shall add that the heads of the shrimp were still on; and not just the heads; the legs, eyes, fantails. I suspected the country my mother came from didn't bother with daintiness.

My mother began twisting their heads off, tearing off their rigid pink bathrobes, and eating their soft curved bodies. Ursula reluctantly put her hand in the bowl. I lifted a specimen up by a long antenna and left it to rest in peace on my plate. My mother liked seafood so much, she rarely complained about our pickiness with it. The price per pound was high, even if she didn't buy it in a store, but on the peer, as bait.

When Cecilia served the main course, our mother's chin lifted habitually: rump roast, cream of wheat with sesame oil and thyme, mashed sweet potatoes with finely chopped raw onions. I pressed the cream of wheat through the prongs of my fork, and made a deep criss-cross design. Meat was rarely too hot to put in the mouth, though I often acted as if it was; if it could not prevent my eating it, it could at least delay it.

"Kate. Eat you meat. You need de red to replace what you lose."

"With teeth like that, Olga, you know she'll never get a man."

I made a face to show them I didn't want one, which amused, of all people, Ursula. It was the first time she laughed all day.

"You know the Minsky girls are getting them, too. Rosa and Lucy. Braces are really a must these days."

"Please, Ursula, stop. You are ruining my appetite."

Someone who hadn't grown up with my mother might not understand what she meant, might think she simply shunned all that was related to the teeth, or those forlorn days with a man. I, her eldest child, could explain. My mother had thought that braces were going to do most of the work like an electric hedge-trimmer and that it would be like buying one at K-Mart on sale for $19.99, for braces were not even a handful of stainless steel, when you can get a casserole for under five bucks. She had not been prepared to part with two thousand dollars of hardworking money for abstract dental services. For that price, one could purchase a used vehicle and in her mental balance, a used Buick versus a palm full of metal bands were no more comparable than a feather and a lead-heavy life of sin. My mother would never consider an orthodontist's know-how as work, as he did not sweat. The consultation which started out friendly enough had ended up otherwise, and *that* was what was ruining her appetite.

"De damn crook. He wan's to cheat me, all 'lone in de world wit' two chil'ren, two tousand dollars, an' on top, he tinks I have nothin' to do dan go over de bridge, back an' fort', one hour ev'ry week, de traffic, my gas, den wait more hours of my precious time so he can take her five minute an' look in her mouth to say ev'ryting is a'kay?! Fin' another sucker!"

Ursula watched me block my nose to swallow my meat. I used my milk as mouthwash.

"Olga. You can't do that to the kid."

"Why not? She can eat with dem. If she don' eat, it's not b'cause o'her teeth, it's b'cause her stubborn head."

"Look at her. Just take a look."

"An arm an' a leg for a few stupi' teeth??"

"Olga, there's no price. It's unthinkable! Come on, she's your *daughter*!"

"Do *I* need them? Look."

Cecilia clenched her teeth together, and spread her lips

wide, exposing her Hallowe'en pumpkin smile. In her enthusiasm, she'd forgotten what was in her mouth and a small piece of beef filled the space where the front teeth normally were. At first, I mistook it for her own tongue, for it blended in so well with her gums and the lining of her lips.

"We are a' de table now, not de dentis' office! Cecilia?! Shut you mouth! It is time to eat!"

We continued our meal with heads bowed in silence, though it was not really silent; it was rich with the familiar sounds of eating. Even the silence was in a way loud. It always was when my mother had just shouted.

"Who wants more?" my mother threatened.

I spoke up first, "Not me. No thanks."

"I do. Well done," Cecilia requested.

Ursula held out her dish. "I'll take a little piece from the middle, please, if you can find something rare . . . "

My mother carved a generous portion for Ursula off the flat red end, when a thought of Betty's posterior entered my mind.

I never should have thought that. I put it out of my mind immediately. Quick, I had to concentrate on something because I could feel the thought was coming back. I thought of a toothache, icebergs in Antarctica, my dead grandmother, the pool filter that had to be emptied, but the thought of Betty's buttocks returned as predicted, and the more I chased the thought away, the more it returned with gusto. The tingles were like tiny fireworks, pulling my attention more and more to them, pulling the blood out of my head, and down to that inglorious crossroad. I couldn't understand how buttocks could trigger off such a reaction, make my blood change its very course. Naked human buttock used to make me *scream* with laughter. If Laurel or Hardy's britches dropped, that would have been the end!

"Stop that this very instant!" I ordered myself.

To my surprise, my body answered me, it answered me with

an unexpected wave of, what can I call it? Concentrated sweetness?

It was with distaste that I noticed my underwear was wet; a baby would have had to be changed, but in my case, it was my second mouth that had begun to drool, to hunger. *It* wanted to be fed. I looked at the roast on the table. That wasn't it. I closed my eyes and Betty's copious behind popped again into my mind. So did Harry's. The way he moved it to some inaudible beat when he was sloppily consuming Ursula. I thought of Belinda Moors' breasts. Why were domes of flesh all at once, out of the blue, so bewitching? They had always been so pitiful before; ludicrous outgrowths, obnoxiously protruding humps, human hills that made you simultaneously laugh at and feel sorry for an adult.

"Mótina, may I be excused from the table?"

"Wha' for?"

I hadn't thought of that.

"I have to go to the bathroom."

"You can't contro' youself?"

I shook my head miserably.

"Den hurry up."

There was a golden oval tray on the dressing table in my mother's bedroom. On it, one invariably found an imitation turn of the century brush, mirror and comb set that she had purchased for twenty books of green stamps many years ago, orderly arranged on either side of a powder compact like a fork, spoon and knife. I locked the bathroom door, sat down on the toilet, leaned forwards and backwards with my arms hugging my abdomen, but the sensation was not going away.

I took in a deep breath, prayed to God for courage, and with my mother's mirror sought the source of agitation below. At first, I couldn't believe my eyes. I consulted the other face of the mirror until I was sure a trick wasn't being played on me. The two tender lips of my childhood had opened like a steamed clam and in-between, an excess growth of newborn flesh similar to a turkey's crest ostentatiously proclaimed its status. Its colouring was that of a rooster's comb. Multiple folds gave it the look of a sluggish, defenceless mollusk, just homely enough for people to consider a refined morsel, much like escargots, mussels, oysters and other bite-sized, boneless seafoods for which they are willing to pay great sums.

The crest separated into two smaller flaps, well done and crinkly like bacon around the edges. I moved them up and down like airborne wings, stretching them out to their full wingspan. They were covered with permanent goose bumps which was proof that the material for this part originated from the plucked members of the fowl family. A small patch of hairs had grown nearby, curly as a lambs. The outer lips were browned at the edges as though they had undergone a light roast in the oven. I opened them like a dissected frog. I knew it! The inside was less cooked! It was exactly that red called medium rare, like the roast beef I had eaten on Thursday night. There was a brown opening to the very back, well done and stringy like the veal I'd also eaten not so long ago at Ursula's. How fascinating: below, one found patches of the exact same skin as that which lines the interior of our mouths; not surprising, then, it was constantly feeling something similar to hunger.

The more I looked down at the mirror, the more I found the composition prehistoric. It was the skin and flesh of seven animals without the brains of a single one; if they were under *my* brain's jurisdiction, it certainly didn't show. I removed a needle from a Holiday Inn sewing kit and gave each meat a prick. I couldn't believe it. Each prick hurt *me*! So they, all seven distinct fleshes, were *me*.

I hoped baptizing it would help and drew a palm of cold water from the tap, sprinkling it with the hopeful drops. At first, it did quell the hot tempers, but soon enough the beastliness resumed. I flicked it with a comb. It made *me* jump with pain, but *it* throbbed and enjoyed the attentions all the more.

My fingers curled inwards like a cat's paw, digging nails into my palms; my toes tried curling under in a similar manner, as though my feet were turning into bird claws; my head was thrust back; whatever was overtaking me didn't need my head around to think. My jaws clenched: it was not that mouth that wished to be fed, despite the hungry grunts that escaped from it.

It wanted to be fed. Didn't it have all the ingredients it needed? Egg, yeast, Jesus' bread, my blood that I could feel pounding down there. How could it ask for my husband's meat if I had no husband? It didn't care what I said or thought, it didn't care one bit about me. It was a composite monster, drooling at the mouth, beckoning me for my hand. One cannot imagine my fear and abhorrence when I witnessed my hand disobey me and descend towards it. My poor hand was going to be bitten right off! I just knew it! Or even worse, it was going to be sucked up into it, or merge with it, and I wouldn't be able to get it away! How would I explain such a thing to my mother?!

I despairingly tried to fool the uncouth, salivating creature by touching it with a lint brush that was in the drawer next to me, in lieu of my hand. It moved! To my amazement, it accepted it, and gave the lint brush little kisses. It was almost cute, and yet it was not. It was simply as touching as any weakling is when in need of nourishment. It had no teeth as of yet; only the soft lips of an innocent baby that puts everything and anything in its mouth. I must not let the innocent baby parallels fool me, I warned myself. The hunger spells of babies are by far the most tyrannical.

I closed my eyes. The pleasure increased until it could increase no further. My arm dropped limply, anchoring me back to reality, and the lint brush fell to the floor. I was freed of the curse, I was rid of it.

Before returning to the dinner table, I ventured nervously to the medicine cabinet mirror, the model with three doors one can adjust to see oneself at every possible angle into eternity. I expected to see sparks in my eyes, two horns sprung out of my head, perhaps even a fluffy tail. I saw no blood-curdling transformation, no horrific signs of catastrophe, only that old familiar me.

I washed my hands with hot water and soap. I had trouble looking my mother, Ursula, and Cecilia in the face, so I concentrated on the meat left on my plate, cold and stiff like me. That's when a lump began to form in my throat. I asked for more milk, but it didn't help it go down. My mother treated my embarrassment with compassion. She promised to make me rice the next day.

CHAPTER 13

A green pea shot past my head. The cafeteria had turned into a battleground and the floor was covered with flat green casualties. Green plastic soldiers didn't die like green peas did; they just fell over and were ready to start over again. The pint cartons of milk were assaulted with straws until bubbles rose high out of them like bunches of white grapes. Chicken legs and thighs were twisted and cracked apart, a few bites taken, and left to the side. The dishes had divisions for each food group, much like a TV dinner. There was constant bartering, especially for a second helping of dessert. I don't know what was most unbearable to me, the table manners or the screaming; I ought to have been grateful for the screaming; it covered up a more hateful noise, that of mass eating.

Needless to say, my mother wasn't willing to pay hardworking money for "dat junk". The first year we moved to Wachovi, she filled out a form for free lunches and free milk and was furious when her application was refused. To her, the title "unemployed widow" should have been enough to kindle charity in the heart of the nit-pickiest of American bureaucrats. When she filled the form out the following year, the zeros dropped like flies off her assets, property values, bank account balances; the number of her dependant offspring rose as radically. She claimed she had had three children before us in Lithuania. She said the school would never check up on that, and it was true, it didn't. We were given hot lunch coupons, but went without eating half that year because the shame of being stigmatized with the red, white and blue coupons was too great. When my mother received a phone call from Mrs. Washington, the school principal at the time (Mrs. Washington was black, and had been transferred to our school during the bussing crisis) informing her that Cecilia and I spent our lunch time outside reading books instead of eating, and wondering if she, an active member of her church, Methodist or Baptist or one of those denominations, could personally be of any assistance to us, we were given lunch boxes from then on with my mother's homemade concoctions. We never admitted to our mother that we were ashamed of the hot lunch coupons; we simply told her the food they gave us in school wasn't good.

The war degenerated and someone made a flame thrower out of a pint of milk and a straw. I walked around a few green smears and did my best to fit in wearing my new dress, known in school as the Bell, a flowery thing that kept its all-weather puff thanks to a hula-hoop sewn into the bottom hem and had a square low-cut collar, front and back. You could wear it either way, it didn't matter. You walked, it rang.

All I would have liked to do was sit down; you'd think sitting down was the easiest physical activity humans can do; sitting down doesn't take ten years of daily practice, wasn't some great feat only Houdini could do; but sitting down necessarily meant sitting down next to somebody, and *that* was not as easy as one might think in a middle school cafeteria. Every chair was supposedly taken, or being saved for someone else. If I insisted, those seated began to shift around and squeeze me out, a round of musical chairs. I felt like a gypsy with her hand out, in tattered rags, begging for money at a benefit ball. In physical education, whenever teams were being chosen for softball, I always ended up the last one, the one left over, the one whose name wasn't called, but one team *had* to take, to the delight and laughter of the other. Every school has one of those. I was that one.

In class, I was the other one; the one whom peers fought tooth and claw to sit next to, the one they edged their desk towards. These friendships were short-lived; approximately one hour, the duration of the exam. If I tried to walk next to anyone after class, she or he usually stooped to untie a shoe.

I wandered outside into the courtyard, opened my new Bedknobs and Broomsticks lunch box (Ursula's Christmas present to me; in exchange, she received the gingerbread Cecilia got in school), and took out my Bible I was recently in the habit of hiding in there. What was happening to me was not only normal, it happened since Adam and Eve. Fleshy desires were one of the Bible's central preoccupations.

The Adam and Eve passages fascinated me the most. A few days earlier, changing classes, I happened to bump into my old teacher, Mrs. Wella. I pointed to the lump I felt in my throat and asked her if she knew what it was; it so happens she did: it was known as an Adam's apple. I started noticing every Adam's apple I walked by.

Stacks of chairs were lined up against the wall. The rolling belt continued its way to the kitchen like a segmented creature, without a dirty tray left on its back. It was time for me to go. I put my Bible safely back into my lunch box, and left my beef tongue sandwich for the birds and ants.

The Wachovi News Press came to our gym class that day to take pictures of the kids who had won Presidential Physical Fitness Awards, a big deal in our community, because the winners received certificates with photocopied signatures of Richard M. Nixon. The repressed giggles were like crumbs left here and there in a dark evergreen forest, nudging me on in the right direction. I found my dress lining the netless basketball ring, upside down, and filled with our gym's reserve of basketballs. The hula-hoop sewn in the bottom hem kept it from falling through, though the weight of ten or so basketballs bent it sharply in two like the hinge and dual arc mechanism of a pair of jaws. It was quite a sight: my gown so altered, multitudes of bumps and domes molding the fabric into someone else; it was the incarnation of my subconscious; a surrealist sculpture of surplus breasts and buttocks. I hurried to find a chair I could reach it with.

Cecilia and I had the habit of meeting at the flag after

school so we could get a seat on the bus together; we weren't unduly patriotic or anything; we pledged allegiance to the flag every morning in school like everyone else, and that was the extent of it. My mother, like most naturalized Americans that were once Eastern Europeans, had been accustomed to outbursts of nationalism; I deduced this from the way she waved a flag around during the fourth of July parades in this country: feverishly enough to make people around her wonder if we had just won a war. And not just any flag, no, no, no; the last page of the Wachovi News Press where the American flag was printed on one side only, for children! On the other side, were the answers to the crossword puzzle of the day before, the horoscope forecast, and the comic strips. She waved *that* around on a yard stick, yelling "God Bless Amer'ca!" and "Long Live Yuncle Sam!" until Cecilia and I acted like we didn't know her.

Cecilia was nowhere in sight; considering how late I was, I guess that was predictable. I made haste, cut across the grass, nearly tripped over a low, draped chain, and had just gotten on the school bus when Barry Ramsey pushed me off.

"Go back in there right now, metal mouth, and put those basketballs right back where you found them."

"I found them in my dress."

"I don't give a crap where you *found* them; it's where you *left* them that concerns me. I'm responsible for the equipment."

"Then take care of it and leave me alone."

"I will as soon as you go back in there and pick them up off the floor. I'm not your fuckin' maid!"

"Nor am I yours."

"You better do what I say, railroad tracks."

"Stainless steel sex appeal."

The reply was Ursula's; it didn't sound like me; nor did it correspond to my looks.

"Don't make me puke."

"You had better let go of me this instant or I am going to tell."

"Be my guest. You're the one who's gonna get in trouble."

There was a small crowd forming around us. A boy I'd seen playing Frisbee in the morning instead of going to class looked at me. The stubble on his face was as long (or short) as his crew cut. I'd seen his name, Winston Bee, carved into the washroom walls. Without warning, he ducked into the tent-like space between my waist and hoop, before rushing out and fanning the air before his nose. He thought Cecilia and I wore the same dress all week and not a different version of the same dress every other day. The crowd encouraged him to more dramatic interpretations. He staggered before fainting and underwent an epileptic seizure.

The buses had started. I made a pathetic run for it, the two yard dash in seven seconds. Barry had caught me by my hair, his eyes squinting down to hateful slits. I felt something almost gratifying, I know this will sound absolutely preposterous, as if I were a fish about to be eaten.

"Your ass is going back in there now."

His Adam's apple went up, and down. The more he squinted, the more I found myself looking up at him with strange sleepy eyes. An apple core was stuck in his throat; a bite of knowledgeable fruit surrounded by weak flesh, like a sweet baked apple in the snout of a roasted pig.

My back struck the earth's crust. At one point, I saw Cecilia kicking Barry in the head. Really, it wasn't as bad as it sounds, for she was wearing my old, soft leather sandals which were only kiddy size thirty four; still I was moved; it's the thought that counts.

Mr. Liverpool rushed towards us, led by our octogenarian bus driver, Mr. Ginger. Everyone turned around to watch him run. Mr. Ginger had been the talk of the town for the past two years. Some said he shouldn't be allowed to drive a bus at his age, that he could have a stroke at any minute. Others said his medical exams showed he was as fit as any forty year old man. The letters to the editor that the Wachovi News Press was only too happy to print were getting more and more below the belt, until Mr. Ginger made the front page by swimming four miles across the bay, towing a row boat by his real teeth. After that, no one dared say a word any more. Personally, I would have given him a psychological exam.

Barry was holding his Adam's apple. There was nothing of an apple at all in there, only cartilage and meat! The apple's skin was clearly human skin, and the apple's juice was recognizably warm and red. Segments of thin lip skin dangled in my mouth like that fine outer skin of a peeled onion. My new braces had grated my inner cheeks like a Parmesan shredder. When my mother heard on the radio that overbites could cause migraines later on in life, she had finally given in. Before Mr. Liverpool had quite reached us, Barry tackled me again.

Barry, Cecilia and I were suspended from the school bus for the remainder of the year, such was Mr. Liverpool's verdict after weighing each of our tearful versions and wounds. He saw that my front tooth was chipped. (It had been chipped against the driveway years earlier, but if Barry's pulling of my hair didn't show, I was forced to substitute it with something else.) Barry had a bite mark around his apple. The gap at the base of the throat between the clavicles swelled outwards like a blood-filled blister.

Mrs. Ramsey picked up her son with the silence and rapidity of one accustomed to his behavioural problems. Once again, Mr. Liverpool dialled our number. I never should have told him where my mother was.

When they arrived, I think my mother wasn't aware that she was still holding onto her bowling bag, nor that one of those one third fractions of a pencil you get in bowling alleys and Yahtzee boxes was still behind her ear, squishing a soft, blonde curl. Ursula nodded to each of us apologetically, as if she had just barged in on a sacramental service because she'd opened the wrong door. They listened to my side of the story, which was the filtered truth, but my mother's face flushed so excessively that I found myself continuing my descriptions more mildly.

My mother confronted Mr. Liverpool, "So! You! Why you punishin' my daughters?!" Her index finger was like a dagger ready to stab him in the face.

Mr. Liverpool explained how we were to serve as examples that you do not take authority into your own hands.

"You hear her! De boy, he was both'ring her! An' she, she defen' her sis'er!"

Mr. Liverpool was the frail, pallid Protestant type, with white hair and a three piece suit, who had never yelled or been yelled at in his life, even as a child. His strong principles made him insist that I should have gone to a superintendent for assistance.

"Someone, dey attack you, you wait 'til you are murder-ed dead to go to de super tendant??"

"Yes, Ma'am."

"You do? You wait 'til you are murder-ed dead?"

"Yes, Ma'am."

Mr. Liverpool returned his face to his paperwork on his desk so my mother would get the hint it was time to leave. He pulled a ballpoint pen out of a tight bouquet of pens and pencils; paper-clips thrown in here and there were stuck between the wooden and plastic stems like petals.

I don't know if my mother was trying to prove her point or to simply vent steam, but she rammed her bowling bag into Mr. Liverpool's back, repeating mercilessly with each consecutive blow, "Now wha' you do! Now wha' you do?! Eh? Eh? You call a super tendant?"

Mr. Liverpool, understandably outraged, for enclosed in that red, white and blue segmented leather bag, was a fourteen pound bowling ball, stood to demand, "Leave this office immediately!" He trembled uncontrollably, which made him look a decade older in the span of a minute.

"Olga, please, calm down you, calm down you," pleaded Ursula, thinking that maybe if she resorted to my mother's syntax, her words might sink in more.

Cecilia acted as if nothing were going on. How one ought to behave was to her nonsensically abstract. She took people for the way they were and never expected variations of thought or temper from them. Cecilia, I thought, would make a good wife.

"I pay for dis office, it belong to me as much as it belon' to you! Who you tink you are?!"

My mother did everything she could to get out of paying taxes, yet everything public, I noticed, belonged to her. She crossed her hands over her abdomen and concentrated.

"Mom!" I exclaimed, fearing the worst was to come and it did.

"Mótina!" gasped Cecilia, even she blushed this time. I guess as my mother's own flesh and blood, she felt somewhat organically responsible for what had just occurred.

"You wan' I do again?"

My mother now defied all of us in the office and I think she did try indeed, aiming her posterior towards Mr. Liverpool who had taken refuge behind a waste basket filled with reams of yellow legal paper.

Mr. Liverpool quietly mentioned that if I were too indisposed to seek help from a school authority, that Cecilia easily could have, and it was not proper conduct for a school-girl to have kicked a fallen boy in the head. With that, he gently asked if he could be of further assistance to us.

My mother said, "Yes. You keep you big words to youse'f."

Outside, our mother gave us a choice. Feeling that she had already paid for our public transportation in her income taxes, the ones that she deducted to nearly zero the last few years, and thus unwilling to repay a supplement for car fuel, either we had to ask Barry Ramsey's mother if she would give us a ride to school with him, or get up at five in the morning and walk.

Cecilia and I chose to walk.

CHAPTER 14

"To my biby I am prou' of, you work very har', you deser' wha' you get."

My mother lifted her glass and, it almost goes without saying, her chin in the air. Fishing nets were strung up on the walls around us as though we were part of the catch, (clients, or suckers as my mother would put it when she would have to pay for anything). One dollar bills with signatures on them were tacked on the wall behind the cashier. My mother looked at these with distaste.

"I hope you order-ed wha' you wan'. It's de las' supper."

"The last supper before she goes," protested Cecilia, "You make it sound like she's gonna die."

"Wait an' see. She's goin' to ge' so smart, she's goin' to forget her Mótina."

"The wisdom of this world is foolishness with God," I quoted.

"Tell me, Kate, honey, from de ten tousand dollars dey give you, you get sometin'?"

"No, Mom, I already told you, it shall cover all my expenses, but I don't get any cash in the palm of my hand, no."

"Yes, but say you don' go?"

"I will go."

"Yes, but jus' say you don', you get to keep de money?"

I saw what she was getting at and felt indignation stirring in me.

"The goal is an education, Mom, not monetary gain."

Cecilia cut in, "I thought 'the wisdom of this world was foolishness with God?' "

"Yes, but you don' eat very much, do you get some o' de scholarship back for dat, I hope?"

"The cost per meal is the same whether I eat big or small amounts."

My scalp was sore and my eyes felt almond-shaped. At dawn every morning, I took three strands of my hair, one for the Father, one for the Son, and one for the Holy Ghost, and entwined them into oneness.

"Den you be smart an' eat!"

"Yeah, eat! You!" Cecilia imitated our mother with her top-lip curled under so that one could see the gums; she poked my cheek harder than my mother had.

The waiter came back with three plates balancing on his arms.

"But wha' are you suppose to become? I don' understan'?"

"I have requirements to fulfil from the college of arts and letters, and from the college of math and sciences. By my junior year, I'll have to confirm a major. I will at that time commit myself to theology."

"Yes, bu' wha' job will it bring? You?"

"What do you want to be?" asked Cecilia.

"I don't quite know," I gave my braid a tug.

"Den why you waste you time in school instead of to take de ten tousand dollars! You people, you go to school, you so smart, I don' understan', you so stupid!"

"I have two years to decide."

"Twenty tousand dollar, you know how much furn'ture you have for dat, you keep for de rest of you life?!"

"I'm not a pharaoh. I'm not going to bring furniture with me to the grave!"

"You won't bring books either," smiled Cecilia.

"I am absent in the flesh," I hymned to myself.

"You don' always need so much salt to eat! Cecilia, honey, say a blessin', all o' us we here toget'her . . ."

My mother interrupted Cecilia before she was done, "Don' be a mule head, Kate. You sit in de library where de law students, dey go, an' you marry me a rich man!"

"I don't care for a man," I politely stated, as though I were refusing a piece of lemon meringue pie.

"You'll change, you'll see. Whe' de right one comes 'long."

"He'll have to come along on water before she's interested."

"Dat's wha' we all think, den it's love on firs' sight."

"You mean love on first bite," giggled Cecilia.

"Please, don't worry. I'm not afraid of such things. My studies are what are important to me, mostly I wish to live with God."

"God, forget God! Where He lives, dere is no pain, no hunger, no mis'ry, but dere is also no boat, no swimmin' pool, no colour TV!"

"Mótina!" I exclaimed, my hand to my heart.

"Too much God, an' you're not ready whe' de wolf, he comes to eat de little lamb!" she pointed at me with the prongs of her fork, "an' God, He don' pay de electric bills, de tel'phone bills, de groc'ry bills!"

"Not unless you're the Pope," joked Cecilia.

"God, He make de grass grow, de trees grow, He make you hair grow, but He don' pay for you to cut dem!"

"Oh, please . . . "

"You remember you mot'her, wha' she says to you. You listen, too, Cecilia. Maybe one day I'm no' here to give you, too, good free a'vice. So listen. Whe' you meet de man, any man, if de milk is free, dere is no reason for him to buy de cow. Remember dese words! Dey are golden!"

"So what does he have to do, pay for the milk?" asked Cecilia.

"You milk him!" cried my mother, excited by now, "Either he's goin' to milk you or you're goin' to milk him. If you smart, you milk him!"

"If either of you don't mind, the only thing I wish to drink is a cup of God's holiness, and the only thing I wish to devour, are His Holy Scriptures."

"You should have say so in de firs' place, it would cost me less tonigh'!"

"There's a draft in here with all the wings flapping around."

"Shut you mouths both o' you now! *Eat.*"

CHAPTER 15

I arrived an hour early to get a seat in the first row. Half an hour later, no one had shown up. Nervously, I checked my schedule. Room 241, nine a.m., Old Testament.

I joined my palms for morning prayer, nibbling my tongue until it bled slightly. This, I knew, must be done daily.

At nine, the other students crowded into the last two rows. Doctor Westway strolled in with a cup of coffee, finished his doughnut, and clapped his hands free of sugar. He wore a red and black lumberjack shirt, black jeans, and high-top trainers with no laces. The curls of his hair descended below his collar. He reminded me of an undercover policeman.

With a stifled burp, he asked, "Who wrote *La Dame aux camélias*?"

"Flaubert?"

"Alexandre Dumas?"

"Which one?"

"The father?"

"The son?"

"Who wrote the first doctrine on spontaneous generation?"

"Francis Bacon?"

"I'm asking you. Well?"

No answer emerged despite Dr. Westway's expectant stare. "*The Symposium*?" he scanned the faces of the class.

"Socrates, Plato, Aga you know, Eryxima-whatever, and all them others at the booze party . . ." advanced a muscular individual in army trousers.

Dr. Westway didn't comment on the answer before continuing, "Who wrote the Bible?"

I was the only one to raise my palms towards the sky.

"Yes?"

"God." I rejoiced.

"God?"

"How do you like to be called?"

"Kate."

"Kate. Good. Can you start reading Genesis to us. I hope you'll be using the Oxford revised standard version I put on your reading list." He squinted at the minuscule pocket Bible on my desk.

Having read in the bulletin that Dr. Westway held a Doctorate in Theology from Princeton, I assumed he would like a fervent recitation. My goodwill was short-lived. Dr. Westway stopped me constantly, asked me to go back to different passages until I was confused and had to refer back to the pages of my Bible. The thinness of its pages didn't allow vigorous manipulation, and I lost the corners of some in my haste.

Vegetation concerned him particularly.

I read, "Let the earth cause grass to shoot forth, vegetation bearing seed . . ."

"Stop! What day was that on?"

"And there came to be evening, morning, and a third day, sir."

"What day was man made on?"

"The sixth."

Dr. Westway had me proceed to the second chapter, where I read, "Now there was yet no bush of the field found in the earth and no vegetation of the field."

"Then what happened?"

"God makes man out of dust, or clay, or whatever," boasted the boy in army trousers, hugging himself as if to make sure he was now made out of muscle.

"So if I get this right, in the first version, vegetation precedes man. In the second version, man precedes vegetation. Hm. Did God blunder?"

How dare he postulate such blasphemy. Surely, the confusion must be attributed to the translations from Hebrew to Latin, from old English to modern. I said something to this effect.

"Who else besides me reads Hebrew around here?" asked Dr. Westway.

One student, so gaunt that the Coca-Cola glasses he wore across his face seemed a prank of cruelty, had the force to raise a long finger. The student only pretended to read. I watched his eyes pivoting in the wrong direction, from east to west.

"Is the contradiction there?"

"Yes, it is."

For the next several minutes, Dr. Westway referred to the creation of the earth as the "seven day myth" opposed to the "Adam and Eve myth". I was dumbfounded. Sacrilege was not what I had expected from a college called Trinity. Dr. Westway lectured on the "hodgepodge" of authors of this "bestseller", making jokes about the copyright had the "book" been written today, as though Jehovah and Job were mere "characters".

"This is not a book!" I snapped.

There were a few snorts of accord.

"What is it then?" Dr. Westway asked me.

I stood up to say, "Jehovah God is the heavenly author of this sacred library of six and sixty testimonies."

The applause was meagre, but there.

Dr. Westway stated, "I might as well make it clear, this class has nothing to do with belief in God. You are all free to believe or not to believe in whoever or whatever you want, I don't give a damn. This class is about a book, some parts are magnificent, others are trashy literature, blatant propaganda, some of the ideas hold true today, others are long outdated, some of the authors had talent, others stank. If anyone has a problem with that, he or she is free to withdraw. Drop/adds are until Wednesday. No one'll ever know you were here."

As I walked out the door, I stumbled.

I turned the knob quietly and before I even stepped in, found myself the concern of an entire population of faces.

"You must be Lester, Kate. There's one seat left over there."

My neck sank into my shoulders as if a meek bearing could quiet the sound of my steps. Professor Ranji scratched the formula of an amino acid onto the chalkboard. He looked at me peculiarly before writing GLUTAMINE. He added glutamine onto leucine, proline onto serine, valine onto tryptophan. The amino acids linked like chains.

Dark hairs covered Professor Ranji's knuckles. Like air plants, hair trailed out of his ears and nose. His eyes, dark and a trifle protruding, were protected by thick brows. His untidy beard framed teeth as white as any sun-bleached clam shell, and so straight, they seemed filed that way.

Professor Ranji began his lecture, "There was no life whatsoever on the young earth; for over a billion years, it was covered with boiling water, you can imagine the steamy vapours, the moist heat . . . but no life . . . no life whatsoever . . ."

He continued, "The early conditions of the earth can be simulated in the laboratory, hydrogen, water vapour, methane, ammonia, heat and electrical discharges break the gas molecules down and they re-form in these very organic molecules we have been talking about. Scientists call this period on earth, lasting a few billions years, primordial soup, oh, just fancy jargon for chicken broth, you know, water, amino acids, simple proteins, harbingers of the first living cells . . . Um, yes, Kate?"

"You mean to tell me that the origin of life is the birth of protein?! The miracle of life is but a fatty acid? The first living organism but a simple cell already concerned with assimilation?"

Professor Ranji smiled. "The living and the non-living are made up of the same elements, so to speak. One of the characteristics that separate the living from the non-living is the capacity to steal energy from the environment and transform it to its own use."

I clamped my arms between my knees so they would not be seen shaking.

"Then the definition of life is: an edible, that eats?"

"Depends on what you mean by eat. All forms of life do not have mouths. Autotrophs steal their energy from the sun, you know, photosynthesis. You and I can't do that. Edible for some doesn't mean edible for others, look at the detrivores, you know, worms, maggots, vultures, hyenas, it seems they steal the scraps no one else wants."

"So no one escapes the soup??"

"It depends what you mean by *escaping the soup*?"

The chairs of some of my classmates shifted in boredom.

"Sooner or later, everyone eats. Sooner or later, everyone is eaten. If you're not eaten when you're alive, you're eaten when you're dead. So no one escapes being eaten. It's just a question of time."

"The first law of thermodynamics: energy can be changed from one form to another, but it cannot be created or destroyed."

Notes were unanimously taken, for the verbatim law interested my classmates more than did its dire consequences.

Professor Ranji was inspired; he defined other laws of thermodynamics and assigned the chapters of a heavy reading assignment before darting out of the classroom.

"Professor Ranji!" I cried, forcing my way through the slow moving students after him. I reached him as he was opening his office door. I'd never seen so many paperback books in my life. There were glasses of leftover juice on piles of books, tall piles, short piles, you could hit each one with a spoon and make a tune. The walls were covered with shelves, the only place free of books, and consecrated to carvings of a smaller elephant within a larger. There was a plastic flute and a rubber cobra on the floor, maybe a child's because there were also a line of fallen Dominos nearby.

"Professor Ranji?" I mouthed gently.

The first thing I noticed when he turned around was a pattern of black points on the tip of his nose which upon scrutiny proved to be razor stubble.

"Professor Ranji. I'm sorry to bother you, but there are two questions still troubling me. I would not like to die without knowing their answers . . ."

"Well, I hope I can be of help and well before then." He crossed his arms and smiled.

I heard myself which is always annoying, "Biologically speaking, it took two parents to make you, and your two parents had parents, which makes four, and these four had parents, which makes eight it took to make you. If we kept going, we get to 16, 32, 64, 128, 256, 512, 1024, 2048, 4096, 8192, 16384, just to make you."

My ability for basic arithmetic was slowing, so I did not go on further though logically, I should have, for these far-off relatives did not come into being by spontaneous generation.

"Okay . . . " he stroked his beard, pulled down his thick, curly moustache and turned over his lower lip.

I detected the impatience in his eyes and accelerated, "Well the same holds true with all of us. Which means, mathematically speaking, the former population must have been much greater than the present population."

"Are you promoting colonization from another planet?"

"No, sir, I'm not. According to the Bible, we come from two people only, Adam and Eve, so the sum of people it took to make each of us must grow smaller as we count back . . . the former population must be less than the present over-population, according to God . . . " My voice weakened on the last words.

Professor Ranji looked startled; he blinked his eyes slowly.

"Don't tell me you take all that biblical folklore word by word?

"No, no, no, of course I don't . . . word by word . . . " I twisted my braid around my wrist until it hurt.

"Every civilization made up stories to explain natural phenomena, you know. That does not mean even they took them literally. You know that? Science has the strength to admit what it doesn't know, that doesn't mean we've proved God does or does not exist, but a bearded man in the sky looking down at us sounds a lot like what humans would invent."

I felt tears swelling in my eyes and looked down. His wedding ring was blurry. So every cell of my flesh was irrevocably made, to feed, to consume, to engulf. Individually, they shimmered, I could feel them starting up one by one, tingling for his own tasty cells, their protoplasmic sauce of life. I imagined boiling an eye of his, white and brown spotted like a billiard ball. The moral dam holding the current back for so long was weakening, as were my legs. Professor Ranji sensed a metamorphosis.

"And the second question?" he asked, making it a point not to blink his eyes.

I took in a deep breath, "If what you say about evolution is true, my ancestors are carnivorous reptiles?"

"What we refer to as ancestors are usually the preceeding generations of the same species. But yes, all life has derived from the earliest forms of life."

I found myself shifting my hips slowly from left to right.

"Perhaps we can have a bite to eat together and talk about this more?" he asked.

My heart thumped so, for adult ways were yet unfamiliar to me.

I struggled to keep my voice steady, "Do you like meringue?"

CHAPTER 16

A shopping cart partially barred the aisle. Cantaloupe melons were marked down half price. I rolled them to the side, disrupting a few sleepy flies until I found one at the bottom, a pale sphere whose wrinkly skin I could pinch. I fingered the damp bruises. Cantaloupes have no natural division like apricots, where two flabby cheeks swell on each side. My thumbnail was long and extremely hard, for it had three coats of red varnish. With it, I slit open a provisional crack. Mōciùtė's buttocks lost a thin liquid I caught with my tongue tip. I dropped the cantaloupe into my shopping cart.

A butcher looked down at a slab of flesh and, like an artist, executed planes, abstract blocks of meaning, carefully removing frames of white fat. His working biceps, bulging and slackening, distorted his mermaid tattoo; sometimes she was more woman, at others, more fish.

"May I help you, Miss?"

"Yes, would it be possible to have a rump roast?"

"Sure."

"With some fur on it, please?"

"Sorry?"

"I said with some fur on it, preferably white with a large black spot."

"Fur?"

"The fur only has to be on one side, if the rump roast is too deep a cut, give me something along the back bone."

"You mean *hairs*?" He wiped his hands on his soiled apron, an abstract canvas of chance and skill.

"Yes, that piece of meat there," I pointed to one of his displayed amputations at random, "used to feel. It wore a coat to protect it from cold and hungry gazes. Like mine and yours. Because of it, we are both here today."

"All I have is what you see," he half-twitched, half-scowled, unsure whether I was making fun of him, or he of me.

"Fine. I'll take that one. Many thanks."

Drops of blood forsook the doomed flesh, how they sizzled upon contact with the oven's scalding bottom. I watched through the brown window, flesh converting into food. Small explosions could be heard as the roast spat. Heat, I thought, brought life out of gases, and if extreme enough, heat returns food back to its original gases. Clouds of smoke filled my apartment.

Professor Ranji burst in with wild eyes, wet, combed back hair, gleaming teeth in the dark frame of his beard. He dropped a bottle of red wine in and a French bread across the sink, pushed me out of the way, and with his own down-stretched sweater sleeves went to remove the roast, and not without heaven-curdling swears, for I had not used a pan.

"Thought your place was on fire," he apologized, fanning the air and rolling up his soiled cuffs until his sleeves looked exaggeratedly big and fat above his elbows.

The meat rested on the worktop. The top was scorched, the bottom, raw. With the help of a shoeshine rag, once part of a T-shirt and white, he changed the position of the grill to the middle, and threw the meat back in. After he rinsed his hands, he wiped them on his trousers, and opened several windows.

"Wow, fine place you've got here . . . " he noticed at last.

"Thanks. My mother has this friend whose husband has a real-estate agency, he let us have it for practically nothing . . . practically unfurnished as you can see . . . My mother took in his wife while they were getting a divorce."

At the tone "mother," Professor Ranji shrunk like a probed sea anemone.

"Where do they live?" he asked, as though they could be living in the next room.

"At home. In Wachovi. Ever heard of Wachovi?"

"The truth?"

"It's near Gables Beach . . . a six hour drive from here."

Professor Ranji's beard made his grins animalistic, almost predatory growls. I was getting goose bumps, taking on the skin of an easy prey.

"I get the feeling man and wife get sick of each other after awhile, like pot roast every day no matter how much you change the sauce and the side dish, and at the same time, they can't stay away from each other for good, people miss the food from the country they come from no matter how bad it is."

"That's an interesting theory," he frowned, picked my biology notebook off the floor and used it to fan the other rooms. My hair was impregnated with the incense of parched meat. He pushed through the cardboard boxes and banana cases I intended to use as dinner, coffee, and night tables; without asking, he rolled up the garbage bags on which sand dollars and starfish were drying and left them in a corner; it's true, they smelt rather strongly.

"Wow, that's a fine animal you got there!"

"Where?!"

When I realized he meant Stag Head, I took offence.

"Hunting trophy?"

"Graduation gift."

"Sorry?"

"My high school graduation gift. From my mother."

"Strange idea."

"I asked for him. He's family, lived with us as long as I can remember."

"*Lived*?"

"Well, yes. He *is* preserved. He doesn't eat, wake or sleep, but he still watches over us like Jesus on the cross. Here, take some, with a toothpick."

I held a paper plate out to him. Professor Ranji's head leaned to one side.

"Cute, aren't they?" I asked as his hand moved towards the school of beached sardines, smelly and stiff.

He ignored the toothpick I was offering him and picked one up by the tail. The mouth was open and tiny teeth could be perceived like the bristles of an overused toothbrush. With a roguish sniff, Professor Ranji split the miniature fish lengthwise. Every vertebra of the tiny backbone could be counted. Professor Ranji scratched it out of its intended bed with a fingernail.

Mental disgust transformed into a fierce tingling sensation in the zone of my triangle, where my coarse, beastly hairs stood on end.

"You okay?" Professor Ranji squeezed the muscles over my knee to verify their tenderness, or, maybe, to wipe his hand.

I relaxed my mouth and breathed again.

"I'm hungry as a wolf . . ." he admitted.

I looked him in the eye. He was testing me. Lawn chairs were the extent of what my mother had lent me for furniture. With a foot, Professor Ranji pushed the cardboard boxes between us out of the way, reclined his scratchy lawn chair and dropped the sardine from an imaginary point above him into his mouth. Quite soon, he fished it back out and deposited it in an ashtray filled with old olive pits, adding to the concoction his own spit.

I remembered the cantaloupe and rose; put the plug in the kitchen sink and pretended to give mõciùtė's buttocks a warm sudsy bath.

"You don't need to wash that," Professor Ranji said as he came up behind me.

I handed him a knife, with which he scraped out the tumour of mush and thin cancerous seeds which had killed her, and presented a buttock to me on a paper plate. My legs revelled at the sweetness of the elderly scoops, the alcoholic, musty savour of rottenness. I made no effort to hide it, and he, no effort to hide his distaste. His fingers drummed on the Tropicana box.

Although scientific discussion was supposedly the reason

we were having dinner together, our conversation was limited to small talk. He asked my major, my age, my birthday. Seventeen and a half cut his appetite in two; he threw away his melon half. Like a ritual, I brought the roast to the table and he removed the cork from the bottle. With his hands, he broke the bread in two.

The slices Professor Ranji cut were ample. They were brown around the edges, pinker, then red and shiny towards the middle, quite similar to my own intimate meats. On a culinary basis, our tenderest meats are synonymous with our weakest flesh. It was hardly ladylike, but I picked up a slice with my fingers, rolled it and sucked the juices out. Professor Ranji did not seem shocked by my bad manners. I chewed his index finger lazily before swallowing the hairy, cartilaginous pulp. It descended my esophagus slowly and painfully. Professor Ranji groaned.

He took my head between his massive paws and directed it down. I could feel heat already fusing through his trouser's thin material. I don't know what exactly I expected to find, though I imagined the small eyeless creature would possess fully developed eyes by adulthood and fancied it certainly bore a lethal sting, three horns, or a terrifying beak.

With great caution, I lowered the metal tongue to discover still a protective layer of fabric with a built-in opening so the creature would be free to come and go as it pleased. Through this small outlet, I perceived a great nest of black hairs. To one side, the creature sought refuge, for the bulge in the fabric was unmistakably solid. Of course I was terrified, but I knew there was no turning back as I walked down the plank to the adult soup.

I was dumbfounded. Instead of a living, snarling, thrashing creature, all I found was an inoffensive sausage. Behind the sausage, dangled two meatballs, larger than Swedish meatballs yet smaller than stuffed tomatoes, inside a mitten of raw chicken skin. It did not look as appetizing as I in my most nagging moments of hunger had dreamt.

Was it an outgrowth of former life, an intestinal casing filled with chicken, beef and pork? So I had been accurate in my hunches all along, man grows sausage links. It seemed he had pierced the domed end with a knife point, for greasy juice was seeping out as though it were done, though a profane rawness dominated the underside where a blue vein sneaked up to remind me of the fragile boundary between food and life. I wondered if it would be too terribly impolite to fork it a few times and boil it more thoroughly.

Professor Ranji looked down impatiently. He held the sausage firmly at the base, so firmly it seemed that the casing might burst from the additional pressure, and directed it towards my mouth. I closed my eyes and followed the ways of a snake, whose jaws disconnect in order to swallow its victim whole. The thought of a vein running with insect blue blood made my stomach churn.

"Wait!" I requested.

Hurriedly, I cut a piece of French bread in half, spread mustard upon both crumbly sides, and returned with a jar of relish. Professor Ranji found my enhancements amusing as I teaspooned the small chunks of dill pickle upon his edible. He was curious as to where I had become such a precocious gourmet. I reminded him that even a child can make a hot dog. Apparently, I was not the sole consumer to spice up his morsel.

I dropped the sausage inside the French bread and squeezed it with both hands into a lumpy cylinder, somewhat like a pig in a blanket. Barely had I gotten to my knees, introduced it into my mouth, than Professor Ranji cried out in pain, a pain so acute that tears were forced out of his eyes. The mustard, a moutarde de Dijon, burnt him mercilessly. So it was endowed with feelings, selfish feelings of petty preservation that my appetite would have to overcome if ever the meal were to be taken. I fought to deaden my unnatural sympathies.

He rinsed our first link of sausage in the kitchen sink, but the cold water did it no good. Like cold air can make dough fall, so cold water made his minced meat droop. He presented a cold, sad, limp earthworm in my face. Not even a catfish would bite. This would not do. Offended, I pushed it out of my face like one pushes a wedge of pork fat to the side of the plate.

"Dessert?" I offered.

I removed all of my clothes until I was standing in a pair of red pumps. A meringue floated from me, as light as a feather and angelically white. Professor Ranji pawed at it madly, but each current of air caused by his gesticulation only lifted it higher. He sprang onto the kitchen counter and chased after it. He chased it from one room to the next room, leaping, pouncing, pounding, swearing over cardboard boxes and banana cases. At last, he chased it into the bathroom and closed the door. Standing on the toilet bowl, he switched on the light. The ventilator breathed artificially. The meringue found itself stuck against a noisy plastic disk.

Greedily, Professor Ranji snatched the meringue. Spun by fairies from the finest threads of clouds, it shrank at the dampness of his tongue. It disappeared more mysteriously than cotton candy, leaving no sugary trace or tangible memory of an aftertaste, but gave one the sensation of having seen the world from afar, so afar that subjectivity was freed from the tug of gravity and saturated by the eternity of space. The peace and absolute existence as an inedible was sensed for the duration of one second. In the language of edibles, it is called death.

He returned to me dragging his knuckles on the floor, a primitive man without clothing. Invitingly, I danced for him. I rolled apples and oranges down the lengths of my arms. I threw a banana in the air, and caught it in my backside slit, where it remained despite my erratic movements. I combed my coarse bushy hairs with a fork, but it became entangled in the growth, so I left it like a heathen ornament, and shifted, and twisted, and hopped and twirled. Professor Ranji had little appetite, I guessed by the sceptical look on his face. Perhaps I, too, was in need of seasoning.

Lost, I contemplated the refrigerator shelves. Should I aspire for sweetmeats, with orange marmalade, mint jelly or honey, or was that too nauseating a mélange? I opened a cupboard. Condiments could make him suspect severe limitations in my cuisine, never reaching beyond the hamburger and hot dog. Frustrated, I reopened the refrigerator. In a small Tupperware, there was leftover rice. The solution offered itself to me. I patted it and rolled it into my bottom lips like a cake, and then sprinkled it with soya sauce.

"Sushi?" I gleamed.

Professor Ranji preferred tuna sashimi for he sought my tongue. First he tasted it with his own, then he attempted to lure it into his mouth. It was a trap, I knew. Faced with the dire facts of life, I retreated cowardly, covered my mouth with my forearm, content my tongue was still there. It was clear I, the inexperienced one, must precede in the initial bite.

His lips smelt of stale red wine. His torso, though dark meat, proved tough to my probing fingertips. His earlobes were soft, but he had dabbed a strong temple-like scent, maybe a Hindu cologne, in their proximity and this repelled my intentions. There was little meat on his wrist and ankle. His buttock hairs curled like those of a bucolic beast, and smelt as musty as their cheeses. His sausage looked redder and rawer than ever. I took hold of it, yet procrastinated for the harder I squeezed, the more distinctly I detected a heartbeat inside and pondered whether or not I should club it first with a dough roller.

He placed himself on the hob, one hairy foot on the worktop, the other in an open drawer. Before I knew it, the raw sausage was forced into the depths of my throat. Gagging, I struggled to pull my head back up, but he obstinately pushed it back down. He swung his hips in a way for it to detach and slide on its own down to my stomach. I turned my head in the nick of time, only to receive it like a spoon of baby food in the cheek. It was the worst predicament of my life. I didn't really want it anymore. There was nothing tasty about it at all. Nothing to make such a big fuss about.

With a groping hand, I switched the hob on high. My stomach growled at the smell of his buttock hairs warming. I was relieved to know I was normal.

"Take it, take it, it's yours," he claimed, in that diabolic trance I knew too well.

I deferred my aim, gently sucking out a drop of juice here and there, while waiting for the hob to get hot enough to grill at least the skin.

"Yes, yes, get ready, get ready to swallow it," he advised considerately, for it was about to disconnect.

Every muscle in my body tensed as I waited for something frightful to happen. I rolled my eyes up at Professor Ranji. He was sitting there, his eyes shut, his mouth open, panting like a dog locked up in a car, pinching and turning his own breasts like he were fine-tuning a transistor radio. And I leaning forward as though I were worshipping him. The hairs on his body had lost their fluff, totally flattened by his sweat. The linoleum floor was a mess, apples and oranges had run away into the corners, relish and mustard stains gave it the look of a dirty plate.

Eventually, Professor Ranji noticed there was less activity on my behalf. He gave my hair a few brutal tugs as an incentive. That is when he let out a scream that was so loud, it joined the scream of every newborn babe, of every jungle cry, of every animal since the dawn of life ever to be unwillingly eaten. I was overtaken by a sudden rush of gastric juices when the sausage was plucked out of my mouth. Professor Ranji rolled on the linoleum floor, screaming.

A smidgen of skin smoked on the hob, as well as a generous

portion of a meatball. With a knife, I scraped off what I could. Like foie gras, I caked the buttery meatball on a crust of bread and delighted in it. The skin, I picked up by the hairs. It wanted more elaboration. A pinch of salt, pepper, and herbes de provence, and the earth spun under my feet.

CHAPTER 17

Professor Ranji did not come to class on Monday, Wednesday, or Friday. He did not call, send flowers, or write. The first days, recalling what I'd eaten, I felt hungrier than ever and wished for more of the same. The French say, "L'appétit vient en mangeant," and I hold this to be true.

I spent those afternoons marinating Professor Ranji in my mind, in lassi and rose petals. I rolled him in unleavened dough and sharp Indian spices before deep frying him, set his crispy carcass on the sheets of my bed like greasy French fries on paper towels. The very thought of him fed me intravenously with the sweetest nectar I'd ever tasted, that is what made the experience so unique, for I did not taste anything in my mouth, but feeling it in my veins, I knew it was sweet. I was tortured with another feeling, as new to me. It were as if I had left parts of myself behind in his possession, and could not long survive if he personally did not return them to me. I was living, more than knowing it, I felt it. How ironic that in the most heightened moment of my life, I was willing to give my life to him, allow it to be transformed into a food, ready if not begging to be eaten and discarded.

But deprivation curtails appetite and I found myself playing with the sheets of my bed, making turbans on my knees, mummies out of my limbs. I could not believe it; his flesh had been welcomed into mine, yet this meant nothing to him, not even enough for him to pick up a telephone. At first, I found excuses for him, but I had to face the facts at length. Professor Ranji simply passed his meat around to whomever would take it.

Within a week, I discovered that instead of offering me a caloric boost, what little I'd consumed of him was actually robbing me of my usual energies and happy disposition. Basically, it was a tapeworm eating away inside me.

A shiny red Christmas garland was taped around the name tag on Professor Ranji's office door. We were still months away from that time of the year. I knocked vainly with that dull feeling one has when the door already feels abandoned, knowing no one is going to answer, but needing to alleviate the frustration on some object.

"He's ill," the department secretary informed me as she tacked a poster on the corridor wall with twenty-two pairs of dancing X's, some long-legged, some short-legged, all joyous, though none had heads. This miraculous ballet is called "chromosomes".

"Do you know when he'll be back?"

"His wife said not for the time being."

I felt humiliation and sadness stirring in me, until they mixed into one, and I hated him suddenly. He hands out his flesh to anybody. Yet, Christ does the same, I thought. Still, it was different. Could this be what the Bible meant by adultery? Yes, it sounded quite right "adult" – ery.

A fly landed on the corner of my mouth. I hit my face. I blew my nose violently. When I opened my eyes, Dr. Timberland contemplated me with the worried concern a true Christian might feel for one gone astray. In large letters, he had already written SIN on the blackboard.

Dr. Timberland was a disappointment to the eye in comparison with Professor Ranji. There was no meat whatsoever on his face, not even enough for a cold cut. He wore thick black glasses, which from some bony angles made his bleached blue eyes magnify like an eerie hallucination. Deprived of meat and muscle, his buttocks were indented and his legs, arched. His mouth was a vague dash, but when he smiled, the thin line opened and stretched into a large cavity as though his face could be literally peeled off. His teeth were a few millimetres too short, which gave him the benign look of a born vegetarian.

Yes, I thought to myself, he must be popular with women,

and extremely beloved to have achieved a thinness like Christ's. I contemplated him days on end.

I wished for willpower, yes, prayed for the willpower to stop hungering for him. I cannot say that I was never alarmed by the contents of my fantasies. It was always the same. There he was, calculating inside a microwave oven. Behind the door, one could hear the eruption of the mushroom cloud, a blown up replica of his intelligent brain. When he stepped out, his glasses were intact but the skin hung from his bones. His eyes were melted and bubbled like raclette. With my teeth, I scraped off the feverish skin, tender as the foreskin of a newborn child. Particles like fig seeds popped out of the taste buds of my tongue and my raw face burned like chilli con carne.

Dr. Timberland ran back and forth, equalizing letters and numbers, $x = y^2$, $y = 2x - x^2$, sin's and co sin's. A parabola fell down, another stood up, one parabola was large enough to contain a feast of fruit, another so thin that only a stork could have drunk from it. He placed his notes, meticulously handwritten into his briefcase, patted them as if he were putting them to bed; he locked the briefcase with a tiny golden key. He had those long, bony fingers one easily associates with pianists, or artists before they're well known (and well-fed).

I pushed my way to him through a forest of standing bodies and intercepted him just as he descended the podium.

"Dr. Timberland. May I see you a minute in your office?"

I had grown self-confident. I rubbed coconut oil into my legs, sprinkled cinnamon in my arms pits, kept a vanilla bean in my bra and a prune stone in my underwear. That, I was certain, had something to do with it.

Dr. Timberland avoided my eyes, glanced at the door desperately. Four other girls from our class approached him. His eyes shifted nervously left and right, exposing the whites before he left the auditorium. He hurried down the hall without acknowledging our presence. His introverted mannerisms made me feel like we were attacking him, and tempted me, or some impulse deep inside of me, to do so.

"So, what is it?" Dr. Timberland asked me as he entered his office backwards.

"Go ahead, please," I offered the other girls; my generosity was only in appearance; inside, I was worried about my own share.

When they solicited the date of the midterm examination, the maximum days of absence allowed before failing, and where assignments could be left should they ever miss class, one cannot imagine my relief. Dr. Timberland's answers were, the eighth, three, and a nod at the flap in his door.

With prolonged gazes from one to the other, they confirmed their mutual opinion of him and took their leave. I could not help but smile, squeeze my breasts together with the sides of my arms until they kissed and stir my hips around idly.

"And you?" He purposely avoided looking at my body, directing his fugitive eyes to his office walls which were covered with landscape wallpaper. A forest, lush, shiny and green, opened up around us, and a gentle waterfall remained suspended in time.

Without a word, I left my vanilla bean on his desk and walked slowly, silently away. It is better to be mysterious than awkward in such situations. Appetites are as much to be enjoyed as cooking and cleaning.

CHAPTER 18

Dr. Timberland lived in Manatee Haven, the largest mobile home park in the area. From the college, you could get there in fifteen minutes by foot as they advertised, but you'd have to sweat. He did as he stamped down his feet one after the other in his buckled shoes along the sidewalks, brief-case swinging high, its weight pulling him along an extra few inches every other step; only an occasional lizard hindered his otherwise regular footfalls and made him release a pent-up sigh; his suit betrayed his gauntness, flapping in the breeze as if it weren't on a body but hanging on its own on a clothes-line.

Manatee Haven was flat as a board, tidy, green, with white mobile homes; each one had their storybook tree, a driveway with their number written on it, 1481, 1482, 1483, a square of grass, a fake grass doormat with a plastic daisy, a peep-hole. It looked like something you would have played with for hours when you were a child.

Dr. Timberland had a black and white cat named Chess who waited behind the kitchen window for Dr. Timberland to come home without moving, like a ceramic ornament. When Dr. Timberland called him, he forced his head and front paws out of the window, and pulled the rest of himself out with difficulty; the window was open just enough so he could manage doing so without skinning his back. Dr. Timberland picked the cat up by the hind legs and walked him around like a wheelbarrow. They did this every night, and every night when the cat got tired of it, he attacked one of Dr. Timberland's gaunt ankles. It was just a game, after which Dr. Timberland read the newspaper and the cat cuddled up on the discarded pages and was covered with the leisure section.

Before dusk, Dr. Timberland turned on a jet sprinkler to water his square of grass, and sometimes in the manoeuvre to keep the jet perfectly within the boundaries, wet himself. In the evening, he went to check his mail in the clubhouse and dispose of his garbage. Otherwise he stayed at home and, from what I could see, did nothing in particular besides mark papers and watch television. I know all this because I'd been following him around for over a week.

Actually, there were a few things I found unusual, going through his garbage. He went through quantities of chicken broth cubes, maybe ten cubes per day. This tortured my imagination. Everyday I found a gardenia browning at the petals. And almost daily I found an empty bottle of medication for a Miss Paulina Craft, sleeping pills, diverse painkillers. Her name wasn't on his mailbox, neither was "Mr. and Mrs. Timberland". Could "Miss Paulina Craft" be the maiden name of his wife? Was he the one taking her pills? Or was he just throwing the bottles out one by one? Because she'd left him? Was he a widower? I didn't understand. Besides that, he was a normal bachelor.

It was late afternoon. The sun cast a yellow light over the mobile home park. Dr. Timberland was lowering a tin awning, noisy as thunder, over a window that was never lit. I hadn't even begun to approach him, when an insurmountable fear, the kind that slithers up behind you at the onset of dusk, attacked me in broad daylight. My heart beat fast and hard, as if I were about to die.

I'd been brewing him too long in my mind, twisting and turning him, sampling him until he'd taken on unrealistic proportions: the finest, rarest bit, the only portion that could bring me my every happiness. I didn't know yet how self-defeating a one-track hunger could be. Craving for strawberries, one forgets raspberries and blackberries.

I sat down behind someone's tool-shed. A lizard eyed me suspiciously from it. I waited until Dr. Timberland cut a gardenia and sunk his nose into it.

"Dr. Timberland?"

If he looked up with a pleasant enough smile, exposing his infantile teeth, his face fell unsympathetically as soon as he recognized me; maybe he had been expecting someone else, Miss Paulina Craft to come home; maybe it had to do with the dress I was wearing; it was too short. I had told myself I was overdoing it when I'd bought it from the second-hand store, but I thought he'd like it because it was made out of a synthetic stuff, the fur of an animal that didn't really exist. I had blackened the contours of my eyes, grown my fingernails to twice their original length, covered them with three coats of red varnish, shaved the hairs off my legs for the first time, just for him. I was so nervous, I held myself as if I were cold, which was unlikely in my attire; I felt my face sweating; the pressure of my arms against my sides made my breasts swell out of the furry V-neck, but even this didn't appetize him; he glanced down at them with distaste. I was losing all my self-confidence. I could hardly speak. I should never have trusted my voice, it had all the nervousness of premeditation trying to sound spontaneous.

"I'm in your class. Do you remember?"

I knew he knew very well, but he wasn't saying a word, just staring at me in disbelief.

"May I have a minute with you?"

"My minutes, and hours are posted on my office door."

"Yes, of course, why don't I see you then?"

He picked up his garden shears and walked away.

"You don't happen to know where the clubhouse is, do you??"

He pointed without looking back once, a nonchalant flick of his shears. Even if I *did* live there, he didn't care! My face reddened, burnt. The ignominy! Curtailed hunger, unrequited appetite! I ran home, back to my own company, and cried until my make-up left a ghostly portrait of myself on my pillow. Then I ate everything sweet I could find, four cans of peaches, and a box of white sugar, cube by cube. When I was done, I was hungrier than ever.

CHAPTER 19

Professor Ranji returned to class with a limp not worthy of his yellow jogging attire. His face had a chalky complexion and underneath his eyes, were night blue semicircles. His eyes were covered with that glossy film that is often the result of medication or fever. As he spoke, he never allowed his eyes to focus quite on me, concentrating to look just inches in front of my forehead. I crossed my legs. Black stockings do not go nicely with red pumps, I thought to myself, pulling out the wrinkles around my ankles.

Professor Ranji's hands trembled as he walked up and down the rows, holding up a wide-mouthed jar for us all to see. It contained a translucent, offensive smelling liquid and one hemisphere of the human brain, separated from its partner like a grapefruit slice.

When Professor Ranji pointed to the area of motor cortex which commanded the muscles of the lips, tongue and jaw, his eyes at last met mine; not to greet them, but to burn them with his hatred. I must say that if I understood correctly, we do not really taste with our tongues. Our tongues are but civil servants who carry taste up a well-defined path, to the viscous ruler above, the brain, which determines its pleasure or disdain.

It was a curious moment in my life. I felt as though something was shifting inside me, a tide reversing prematurely. I do believe, though it may sound queer at first, that it was responsibility shifting from the low rank organs of execution to my brain. Yes, how curious, the area I'd considered the most moral of myself all those years, in all its scruples and accusations, was the very source of pleasure all the while, a masochistic mass battling against itself.

I couldn't wait for class to finish, and bobbed my knee up and down. As soon as Professor Ranji gave us leave, I rushed out of the Scott's Science building; my heels sank into the grass, stabbing the earth again and again. If I ran fast enough, I could catch Dr. Timberland as he arrived on campus, brief-case swinging high, jacket flapping in the air.

"Hey! I want a word with you!" Professor Ranji was unable to run properly; one leg almost ran, and the other one trailed behind, looking stiff in his jogging pants, as if it had been taken off and put back on the wrong way. I recognized his Hindu cologne that had once enthralled me before he limped up to me, too close for my taste.

"I'm in a hurry. I have Honors Calculus in ten minutes."

"You did it on purpose, didn't you? The whole thing was premeditated, wasn't it?! You don't have to admit it to any goddamned juvenile court, but you're going to have to admit it to me!"

"I don't know what you're talking about."

He shook me by my dress; synthetic hairs floated away, lightly, carelessly.

"What are you, some sort of witch? A Medusa?!" Veins rose out of his moist forehead. He had a plaster on the vein one draws bloods from, surrounded by the usual spectrum of a healing bruise.

"Without oxygen, your blood is blue," I commented and began to walk.

"What the hell did you do with it?!" Panting obstinately, he struggled to keep up with me; every few feet, he scratched the same impolite part of himself. I noticed that the puma on his sweatshirt had a loose, hanging gold bead eye.

"I beg your pardon? With what?"

"The piece I'm missing! You know damn well!"

My hand covered my mouth instinctively, as though I were protecting myself from repossession of what was duly mine.

"You ate it? I can't believe it! You ate it? I knew it. You ate it??" Professor Ranji squatted against a banyan tree and buried his face in his palms.

"Does she know?"

"Who?"

"You know damn well who! Was she behind the curtain, whispering stage directions to you?"

"By *she*, I assume you mean your wife, rather than your mother or daughter?"

"Tell me it was an accident, your elbow accidentally hit the knob, you didn't know what you were doing, you're very sorry, it was an accident, something, but don't stand there looking at me like *I'm* the freak!"

I didn't know if it would be suitable to weep like the heroine in a three-decker novel or to run.

"If you wish to alleviate your guilt for having merged your flesh with flesh other than your wife, confession is on Sunday," I reminded him.

The face Professor Ranji made was so sincerely void of understanding, I conceived my mistake.

"Will, how you feeling?"

I was startled to discover Dr. Timberland standing behind me. My body tingled all over. I now knew it was just my brain having fun, tossing electricity here and there like grains to hungry chickens.

"Hello Stan," murmured Professor Ranji.

Dr. Timberland gave his glasses a few puffs and wiped them on his jacket.

"You all right? I heard you were ill?"

"I'm fine, just fine, much better, this is nothing . . ." Professor Ranji confessed acidly. He started to peel the plaster off his arm, but halfway through changed his mind, and patted it back down uneasily.

"I see Miss Lester is one of your prize students, too?" Professor Ranji looked me up and down, then back to Dr. Timberland with eyes full of warning.

Dr. Timberland was disconcerted. He glanced at me from the corners of his eyes, and thought I didn't see him press his thin lips together to suppress a laugh. I lifted the silver chain out from between my breasts and nibbled on the tiny Christ.

"Why don't you both come for breakfast? Tomorrow is Saturday, there are no classes. Oh, do come??"

"No, but thank you anyway," refused Professor Ranji politely, "I shall have breakfast with my wife and children. How 'bout stopping over, Stan?"

"Is your wife's cooking so great?" I challenged.

Professor Ranji excused himself, lowered his head and dragged his heels to his dusty jeep. When he stepped inside, he did so slowly, straining his face. Before he drove past us, he gave Dr. Timberland another warning stare and uttered, "Bon appétit."

"What was that supposed to mean?" Dr. Timberland asked me irritably, fanning the dust that had risen to his face.

CHAPTER 20

Hunger kept me from sleeping that night. It started out as the hunger that calls one to the refrigerator in the middle of the night, then it grew, it attacked my guts, my sanity. I felt the cross on my breast, a tiny spot of cold. I kicked off my blanket, pulled my dress up over my legs, stepped into my red shoes.

An occasional owl looked down at me from the electricity lines with wide eyes. The streetlights were my only friends, helping me feel I had a right to be out, sentinels whose job it was to help me along the way. I walked on the side of the road without looking at the stars. I knew where I was going.

My feet left prints on the ground, the great island of the heel, the strait to the archipelago. How big they had grown, the feet with which I trod the earth, without my noticing. My footsteps led to a particular mobile home in a particular mobile home park, in front of which was a particular square of grass.

The sun rose over the earth's edge like a Cyclops' eye, a red spot gazing down at me. I stared into it. The red eye heated my tissues, flowed in my body like red wine. The window was open. I only opened it wider, inch by inch, and slid myself inside, head first. I found myself in a dim, narrow kitchen which smelt of cat litter, medication, old people and urine. I landed on a glass bowl of lukewarm water. The cat rubbed itself apologetically against my leg until I went to pet it, and it unexpectedly attacked my fur dress. I stood up in haste, knocking a few bouillon cubes off the plywood board that served as a worktop and was coming loose at the wall.

I only had to cross a room to get to the bedroom. It was small, dim, and smelt of sleep, stale and faintly sulphurous. Dr. Timberland was sleeping soundly, a sleep without the sound of breathing. I recognized the bottle of sleeping pills on a wobbly round table next to him. The sticker read Miss Paulina Craft. There was only one long oval pill left, half white, half red. I pulled the blinds up a bit to see better, and slowly lowered his sheets.

Naked, he was as I had imagined. Besides a tuft of fine golden hairs in the vicinity of his pinkish meats, his skin didn't have a single hair. I could smell the spiciness of his deodorant, and his breath, which was like Japanese broth. His chest is what entranced me. His skin had never seen the sun, and to my joy, had all the whiteness of cooked egg white. His two breasts were like sunny side up eggs, only the yolks, like the sun's eye, were blood red. I turned my head aside and red egg yolks gambolled under my glance. I closed my eyes and they appeared against the soft screens of my lids. Dr. Timberland, how deeply he slept, unaware of the air that moved in and out of him, strangely ignorant of his own heart, meticulous, succulent offal. His eyes, shut, were like ravioli, his eyeballs, bumps of ricotta and ground meat, his lids, coats of pasta.

I slipped back into the kitchen and found a stale loaf of bread out of which I cut five pointed fingers. I found a stick of butter in the old refrigerator (there was practically nothing else besides) and buttered the bread fingers. Three small bottles of spices, white and black pepper, and paprika, stood next to a single hob. I sprinkled paprika over the butter as if I were painting my nails, pushing the cat away with my foot. With five fingers in one hand and a knife in the other, I kneeled beside Dr. Timberland. How both red yolks went up and down with his every breath, as if they were floating on water, the waves moving them gently up and down with the same secret life that animates every ocean tide. With a stroke of the knife, I severed the finest of Dr. Timberland's red skins, keeping me from the tender liquids of his aureole.

Dr. Timberland did not cry. He sat up, looked upon his bleeding breast, and did not move. The red sap seeped down his bony torso, made red canals out of the furrows between his ribs. My mouths drooled all the more. My impatience could stall no longer. I dipped a bread finger into the red aureole and devoured it savagely.

Dr. Timberland, witnessing my act, returned promptly to his sleep before he had even resumed his horizontal position. His head struck the iron bars at the head of his bed with a solemn chime, after which he did not notice, or care, that his neck was crooked, nor that his head was caught sideways between two of the bars. I dipped the remaining bread fingers deeper into the wound.

The bathroom smelt of towels that were never dried properly. The bathtub, I noticed, was sandy at the bottom. I didn't mind. I turned the hot water tap on as far as it would go. The water gushed out, hot and steamy. It was all so exciting. I ran to the kitchen for the bouillon cubes, as many as I could hold, peeled them with joy, and threw them in. I rushed back for a ladle. The bouillon cubes softened, leaving a greasy film on the surface. Chicken soup, I chuckled to myself, mother of life. I ground more cubes with my fingers, observing the water as it turned from lemon yellow to a deeper ochre.

I dragged Dr. Timberland by the ankles. He slid easily inside, into the initial womb of life. I helped him sink lower; he floated to the top; only his head weighed him down, rolled uselessly along the bottom. With my fingernails, I scraped the dead skin off his back, enough to make a bland tasting terrine. Twice, Dr. Timberland attempted to sit up, and twice I was forced to submerge him.

In the broth, his skin adopted a yellowish hue like boiled chicken. I turned the cold water tap on so it would trickle down his feet. The effect I sought was obtained, chicken skin. I remained on my knees, spinning the liquid round and round with the ladle. His member rotated. I scooped it up. On the ladle, the chicken neck twitched from side to side, as beheaded fowl necks are known to do. I seized it, stretched it as long as it would go, tugged and twisted, yet it would not break; on the contrary, each time I let go, it shrank back into the pouch of skin holding the two gourmet lumps, constricting into a more stingy tidbit.

At last, my hunger was fulfilled with a final animalistic spasm; as promptly, my stomach was saturated not with fulfilment but regret. My face reddened in shame as I contemplated the limp form that had caused my countenance to undergo such wild perturbation. Dr. Timberland looked dead floating on his side, and the chicken fat around him had hardened into a greasy yellow crust. Though he was easy game, I was no detrivore. I resented his passivity and banged his head against the bathtub for it.

My hunger abated, Dr. Timberland's home regained the familiar features of any home. At such an untimely moment, one can imagine how startled I was to hear the phlegmatic coughing fit of an elderly person. I could not tell if it was coming from an old lady or an old man; all I knew was it came from the other side of the house. I detected the muffled steps of slippers. Someone was moving towards me.

I hid behind an armchair. An elderly woman with white, thinning hair emerged in an ochre-stained bathrobe down to her ankles, and white gym socks up to her bony knees. She had Dr. Timberland's fleshless lips, faded bleached blue eyes, milk white skin and frail build. She could not walk without holding onto the wall with one hand, and onto her forehead with the other.

"Stanley? Stanley?" Her voice was weak and needy.

The remorse I felt sharpened, gave me sharp pains in my guts. What could I say or do? I ran out, holding my own head with both hands. I didn't close the door or look back.

Night fell, and the impulsive cries of birds and babies were replaced by the snickering of crickets. My hair clung to my neck, as did my hair dress to my body. I could go no further. I wandered into the garden of a hotel and dropped into the first lawn chair.

When I awoke, the sun was teasing me through the branches of the coconut trees. A taste of decomposing eggs was in my mouth. Like a black flower, flies were clustered upon it.

I expected the congregation to condemn me when I entered the church. I was handed a book of hymns and allowed into a pew, but it did not take long for my neighbours' vexation to appear. Each leaned as far away from me as balance permitted, some finding it impossible to stay in the same row. The woman closest to me brought a handkerchief to her nose. Just as onions, garlic, and alcohol cause one to smell abominably the next day, so does gluttony.

I hoped the Eucharist would take away my sins, yet when the moment came, the sliver of Christ's body evaporated on contact with my tongue. I requested a second helping, but was pushed along. Our Saviour continued to bleed on the cross, I heard the blood dripping, drop by drop onto the floor. Jesus was Jewish, I thought to myself, wondering, out of the blue, if His bleeding on the cross had made His meat kosher, wondering if His meat had a sell-by date, wondering if He, in a way, put an Egyptian mummy to shame, all He had to wear for eternity was a loincloth. I rushed out of the church before I could think any more such nonsense.

My feet were bleeding, throbbing in my red pumps; the heels were worn down by running. Dirty, sweating, I was starting to feel like an animal in my hair dress; it was sticking to me like my own skin and the mass of woolly hairs were turning into mine.

Dr. Timberland's front door was unlocked, his window still open, his square of grass still there, serene, tidy, welcoming, as it had always been. For a few moments, I did not breathe. My legs transported me to the bedroom, and the bathroom where it had all happened.

It was as though someone had returned in my absence and the blood that had wet the sheets had been cooked to a welldone brown. The water in the bathtub was cold, and the tint had changed, like the clear water one leaves overnight in a burnt pot.

I looked under Dr. Timberland's bed, lest he, like a dying creature, had sought refuge there. Something stuck to my palm, a flattened raisin. It was not a raisin at all, but Dr. Timberland's dehydrated aureole. I did not know what to do with the wrinkled speck. It repulsed me to have it pasted on my palm. I shook my hand, but it wouldn't fall off. I attempted to flick it away, but the aureole was a malediction, for whichever of my fingers I used for the purpose, it simply stuck to that one's cuticle. Desperately, I wedged it between the iron bars of his bed and the wall, but knowing it was there bothered me. I took it between my teeth, and appropriated it with little satisfaction.

For the first time, I noticed that one of Dr. Timberland's walls was covered with the same landscape wallpaper he had in his office. The pines stood silently, the light shone endlessly, the waterfall was suspended in midair.

The bedroom on the other side of the house was barely bigger than the unmade bed that occupied it, a sulking pile of open bathrobes, knit shawls and quilts. I lifted them up one after the other and shook them, but the old lady, to my disappointment, was nowhere to be found. Old age and sickness left a smell similar to when one opens a dirty dishwasher in the summertime to find room for a last spoon or glass. A reserve of pill bottles kept guard on the barricaded windowsill; I brought a handful of them to the light; all of them were the prescribed medication of Miss Paulina Craft. About a hundred small pictures had been pasted on the wall, mostly of a young skinny boy in glasses and two pretty young women with long, ringlets and bright, all-believing eyes. There it was again, change, that restless drop of water. Not only the contents of the pictures had changed, but the pictures themselves were arching, bending, preparing to flake off the wall.

The kitchen hadn't moved since I last saw it. Only the cat was still there, and for some reason, had not used its litter box the past few days. When I stepped around one of its unclean doings, it rounded its back, backed up under the worktop, and spat at me.

I removed Dr. Timberland's stained sheets and packed them tightly, along with the pillows and mattress protection, into the oven. The bare mattress was also spotted. I longed for cleanliness. I stabbed the mattress and ripped off the coarse, sky-blue material. White feathers twirled up to greet me.

CHAPTER 21

When I finally made it back home after three days of wandering and fasting, I was surprised to find how many dirty dishes I'd left around, leaning against the windows and walls, plates with splotches of past meals. I had no time to lose. I mopped the floor. In the kitchen, something smelly caught my attention, drawing me reluctantly to the garbage bin, where I stood without the courage to open its omnivorous mouth. When I pressed my foot down, the cantaloupe halves from the evening with Professor Ranji were staring up at me, swarming with hundreds of maggots.

I ran to my bedroom and thrust back the sheets. The dry, withered rump roast lay there like a baby which had never grown in size, though had wrinkled with old age. I lifted it by the string and fed it to the garbage disposal. I poured whisky and dropped flaming matches down the drain. I scrubbed the hob until it gleamed. I tore open my mattress. I thought everything was ready and I could finally take a shower and change, when I saw Professor Ranji's footprints on the walls. With a feather-duster, I removed them one by one until I came to Stag Head and, in dusting him, the feathers became tangled in the antlers.

The doorbell rang. I was suddenly overtaken by an uncontrollable anger.

He handed me a particularly cheap brand of white wine I used for cooking, and stepped inside before I had freed the passage.

"Oh, you *really* shouldn't have!"

"Huh?"

Had I not held out my hand, he would not have returned my key to me. I could tell he was too embarrassed to look at me.

"What is that smell on your neck?!"

"Old Spice," he shrugged.

"Remove it!" I ordered, pointing to the bathroom.

He scrutinized me before giving in. When he returned, he smelt the same and I had not heard the water run.

"What're all these darn feathers?" He kicked one weightless pile, then another.

"Angel down."

His manners were drying my palate.

"You ask too many questions!" I had felt another was in the air.

"Then why don't I just leave?" He looked me up and down.

"You must take off all your clothes! You must do as I say!"

"Why didn't you say so in the first place?"

He undid the buttons of his polyester shirt (whatever buttons weren't already open) before their threads burst from his stomach's pressure. Underneath, he was wearing the same tank top he had on at the corner store. He kicked off his cowboy boots next to my ballet slippers. They were crass next to the fragile pink. Their tips curled upwards and the sole detached to give them the subtle smile of a satyr. His socks didn't match, but he kept them on. His white kangaroo underwear might have proved sufficient with a little imagination, but I wasn't inspired.

"I have prepared this for you." I folded a white bath towel diagonally, and set it on the floor.

"What the heck's that for?"

"Sit on it and don't ask questions. Take that off! Bare, I said!" I had to concentrate to keep my voice at the highest volume before a command becomes a yell.

He struggled out of my grip as soon as I tried to stick a safety pin in the towel. I did my best to hold him down, but his knee knocked me in the chin; he was as ticklish as he was clumsy.

"You are no fun!" I complained, crossing my arms over my upset stomach.

"I was expectin' dinner," he retorted sorely.

"You are going to have dinner. But my way."

"I don't like some spoiled brat treating me like no goddamn baby."

I vindictively removed my hair dress to show him what he was missing.

"What the hell'd you wanna do with it anyway," he muttered, toeing the towel.

"If you tried it, perhaps you would have liked it . . ."

"I ain't no faggot, go play dolly with someone else." He lifted one foot up after the other, a brief march, and tore each sock off.

"I'll prepare your supper," I consented, more to escape his presence than to fulfil an appetite he had already spoiled.

When I returned, I was startled to see him pinned in the nappy, his legs in the air.

"Wah!" he laughed until his belly jiggled like a mound of custard one sets down too roughly on the table, "Wah, wah, wah! Is this what turns you on, girlie?" His eyebrows, sparse and grey, established a distinction between his face and forehead, but the transition between his forehead and scalp was impossible to determine, granting him the naive charms of infantile baldness. His stomach was the happy hump of every baby, and his sagging breasts sat upon this hump.

I uncorked the bottle of white wine and dampened his nappy with a minute splash. "Oh, you bad baby boy, you made pee-pee," I wished to participate in the merriment.

"I paid f'r that there wine, now give it here!" he bellowed unexpectedly, wrenching the bottle from my hand and swallowed the remaining contents without inhaling once. When he had finished, he licked the circumference of his lips and burped without anyone having to pat his droopy back.

I don't know what came over him, but he crawled around the apartment on all fours and began going through my belongings. When he discovered the severed mattress, a series of hiccups jarred his slouching, grey-haired breasts.

"You made someone pretty damn mad, I'd say. Do you do this here of'en?"

"Make dinner?"

"*This here.*"

"Dinner is ready." I turned about neutrally.

How oddly he reacted, babbling stupidities: if I was trying to get even with someone, for something, if this whole thing had to do with some ex of mine or some present-day jerk, then he preferred to leave before anything happened because if someone was going to walk in and see him like that, in a goddamn nappy on the floor, his feet up in the air, I might as well know that he was well-known in Pasqua County, owned the corner store for thirty-two years, worth, thanks to no one but him, its weight in gold, had distributors, clients, and a reputation.

I spoon-fed him his dinner to keep his mouth busy, tomato soup, carrot purée, strawberry mousse. The shopkeeper did not consume any substantial amount, rather he took advantage of his role and spat in my face.

"Never cared for it," he coughed, "Not even one year out'a my old lady's legs, I hate rabbit food!"

"Then why do you sell it?"

He let out a second despicable burp and brawled, "So why don't you change my nappy, Mummy?!" When I didn't react, he groped for one of my breasts and said, "I'm thirsty! Got anythin' to suck?"

"That is odd, for you have drunk a whole bottle."

"Fuck the bottle! Give me the real McCoy!"

With his foot, he knocked the globe off my banana case, put it like a pillow under his bald head and spread his knees so I would attend to his needs. I patted his bottom. The nappy was damp with white wine. I inhaled the alcoholic fumes, how keenly they resembled the smell of urine.

"Don't waste no time smellin': suck!" he invited, fumbling to unpin the nappy as fast as he could.

Though I lapped his skin clear of residual moistness, he hardly seemed satisfied. He executed a series of annoyed huffs, left the room and returned with a miniature parcel, the size of an After Eight, but shiny as a candy wrapper. He fumbled to open it, an exploit of diplomatic expertise, how to tear it open like a brute, yet preserve the precious contents. I wondered what quaint morsel could he have the delicacy to transport, imagining a refined rarity.

Whatever it was, it unravelled like a troll's tongue, was transparently pink and at first interpretation, disappointing. Like a dainty stocking, he rolled it upon his member to enhance its natural, faded pink hue. I was astounded at the intricate pains one will undertake for vanity, when I understood its raison d'être. It was a rubber casing equipped with a built-in nipple. What a wonderful gadget, I exulted, recognizing his willingness to play. How clever, out of his impressively stout member, he had concocted a baby bottle.

I drew with force, straining my lungs, but could not retrieve a drop of milk. His face contorted with pain. I excused myself, withdrew to the closet, and removed a needle from the Best Western sewing kit my mother had offered me as a last minute farewell gift.

"What the hell you doin'?" he jerked.

"It's to pierce the point, it won't come out."

"Give it time, lady! An' take it easy with y'r damn rabbit teeth!"

"Shall we boil the nipple for fun?"

"Are you out'a y'r frigin' mind?"

He rolled over to me and put the baby bottle in my face. I was a good sport and accepted it, but again the unpleasant rubbery taste without the recompense of a dairy extract dampened my eagerness after reasonable effort on my part. Not only did my jaw ache, but the more I pumped, the more I noticed his thing grew limp.

I moved it politely aside and he had the nerve to say it was my fault rather than admit the deficiency of his device.

"You're supposed ta suck the whole thing, not just the damn tip! I got ten inches you kin appreciate, ya know, case ya didn't notice!"

If the rubber cylinder were adapted to his piston, agitating the nipple would have sufficed to tap liquid according to the laws of air pressure.

"Main course!" I avoided a fight.

"My dick is on fire," he wailed.

He pivoted himself to expose his profile. It lifted extraordinarily high, I'd say about eleven o'clock, a missile about to take off into the sky.

"I've got something for it," I promised from the kitchen.

"Move it, baby, my balls're gonna explode t'outer space!"

I hurried to him, raised his legs in the air, slid the nappy back into place, then massaged his crotch and buttocks with cream cheese, using my thumbs and chin.

"Whatever gets y'r motor goin' baby doll, make my day, I'll make y'r meal . . ."

I sprinkled on a layer of curry, massaging it to an even mustard colour with my tongue. My mind dwelled on Harry's potty-training problem. An emptiness I'd felt since childhood, a sort of ravenous hunger grew to an excessive state I'd not yet known. I heard hedonistic grunts escape my throat.

"Now yer talkin'," he encouraged, his barometer displaying his corporeal elation.

"Keep on truckin', yeah baby, yeah baby, yeah baby . . ."

I pushed grains of corn into the mess. A fly landed on his buttocks to share the feast. Unfortunately, his skin was tougher than leather; his meat, compact and unyielding so that my jaw ached. All at once, the shopkeeper's body underwent a great spasm. I tried again, this time with all my might. The rage on his face was the last thing I remember.

CHAPTER 22

When I regained consciousness, the globe was inches from my face. I squinted into the paper ocean. The lines, where man attempts to organize the wild seas into handsome squares, wavered and made me seasick. North America was the victim of a dent; it looked as if an asteroid had collided into its flanks, giving it the forced curve of a corseted lady.

My heart had migrated to my head, and every thump gave me pain. When I finally moved, something rolled off my chest and struck the floor with an ear-splitting clink. It was the bottle of white cooking wine with a note inside; it reminded me of a bottle one casts into the sea in desperation. I shook the bottle every which way, but the paper stuck to the side and I was forced to read it through the green glass: "You'r gonna pay bitch."

The daylight shone in through the window and left a blank visiting-card on the floor. With my bare toes, I expected to rake up a ball of dust and hairs, when I started at a clammy texture. I advanced to the thing, my nose practically upon it. It was the shape of a horseshoe, though smaller, and its edges had tooth marks.

I sprang up and threw it in a pot. I couldn't wait for the hob to get hot. The curry rose like oriental incense, a yellow smoke teasing me, intoxicating me. As expected, the hardened cream-cheese slid from side to side, softening, liquefying until it reached a state of erupting bubbles. I scraped and scraped the bottom of the pot with a spoon. I couldn't believe it. There was no meat, no skin in there, nothing!

I paced back and forth, cursed. I put my hand in the garbage disposal. Not even a last string I could chew to get the taste of the roast it had been in contact with. I stumbled around and cursed more. Pulled my hair. Lowered my own finger into the pot and burnt my fingerprint. I sucked my fingertip, reflecting how my own taste differed only minutely from another's.

I set the pot on the floor and attempted to lower my buttocks inside. The pot's edge branded a circle around them. It helped not to insist, I would never get inside. The hob was a glowing red plate. How tempting it would be for me to sit upon it, to smell the aroma of my own cooking meats, to feel them snap and sizzle, to watch the cloud of gases that would rise from them . . . Yes, yes, yes, I would taste a small piece of myself . . .

I rushed out of the apartment, for the occasion was a grand one, and I wished for some uncommon seasoning. I kicked aside every newspaper, flip-flop, and beach-ball that got in my way.

"Where ya think yer goin' in such a hurry?" The voice I heard was friendly.

A woman in late middle-age was sitting on a weathered sack of charcoal, taking in the sun. Her hair was three sorts of blonde, and if this weren't enough variety, her roots were grey. She had on a grass-stained pair of trainers, a tight pair of jeans, a T-shirt and, from what I could see (and anyone else, quite easily) no bra. Her smile was empty, a rag-doll smile with black button eyes.

I assumed she was one of my neighbours and replied, "Just some shopping, Ma'am. Salt and pepper are fine things, but one does need variety in life."

Her smile transformed into a contortion of malice. "You bit my man."

I could not apologize before I knew whom she was talking about. "Which one?" I asked, and not in the least insolently.

"You bite often?" she sneered and came at me with clenched fists. Like the neglected fruit of an overgrown garden, her breasts sagged under their own weight. Although they could feed a famished army, the man to whom she was referring had apparently not bothered to take a bite for many a year.

"My past samples do not concern you unless you have consumed your partner since? I did not think so. Goodbye." I did not wish to dismiss her rudely, but her face answered my questions quicker than her speech did, and besides, I had my own cuisine to worry about.

"So you eat every dick you come across?"

"If you enjoy the same flesh over a prolonged period, I congratulate you. As far as I'm concerned, no piece has yet addicted me."

She blocked my path.

"Now if you shall excuse me." I pushed past her, but didn't get very far.

"You're not going anywhere," she grabbed me, "You bit my husband's ass bad!"

She was breathing heavily; a hiccup jarred her chest and I detected a trace of pork and beer.

"I do not wish to upset you, Madame, but your husband was given the gift of free will from Our Lord above, he consented willingly, I promise you, you shall find no signs of chains or thrashing if you examine him more thoroughly. He should cut the links off himself if serving as a woman's meal, other than his lawfully wedded wife's, tempts him so much."

"He told me all 'bout how it happened, you prick-tease, you was jerkin' off a carrot in his face, you was playin' with a cherry like it was y'r tit, you were puttin' yer mouth on all kinds o'fruits an' lickin' 'em nasty, toyin' with every obscenity you could get yer dirty fingers on!"

As she pulled my hair, I stepped around in an ungainly little dance. "I beg your pardon?!"

"Whadda ya think, yeah gotta go to university ta understand? You all think yer so high an' mighty, yer all ajecated an' smart, well lemme tell yeah, yer more a slut than I ever put my eyes on!"

"Let no man judge you in eating, Colossians, 2–16."

"Don't you play no holy mouth with me, ya nasty cunt!"

"One [man] has faith to eat everything, but the [man] who is weak eats vegetables. Let the one eating not look down on the one not eating, and let the one not eating not judge the one eating, Romans 14:2, 14:3."

"Shut yer mouth, you stinkin' sperm bag!" She gave my head another more forceful tug backwards; unfortunately, she was pulling the silver chain of my crucifix as well as my hair. "Tell me how it all happened, I'm curious t'hear yer vursion. Tell me why ya picked 'im? You knew he had a big one, ya could smell it a mile away, couldn't ya? Was that yer criterion? You teased him 'til you was certain? You was just starin' at it in the mirror, dying t'have it, wasn't ya?"

"If truly you are intent on learning the particularities, Madame, since I was a child, I never was one to clear my plate, so I assure you, I couldn't care less how big the portion is."

I never saw a face so sceptical when hearing the truth spoken. She looked down at my hair dress, crinkled her nose in disgust, and pulled my hair mercilessly. I was certain the silver chain was going to cut my throat, when it all of a sudden broke, and the tiny Jesus fell into the cleavage of my breasts.

"If you'll forgive me, Madame, I left something on the stove . . . and I really must be going . . . "

Grass seeds had been planted around the building, but the grass had not yet grown; normally we weren't allowed to be standing where we were. I looked down and saw my silver chain, long and fine, a shiny scar across the earth, a tiny food chain, a food chain Jesus was an integral part of.

"Don't give me no fuckin' cop-out! I asked you a question an' I wanna answer now!"

"Would you terribly mind restating it more specifically?"

"Why in hell did ya choose my husband?!"

"I assure you, I did not choose him. I did not even sample him. There is all of him still available for you."

"You think he was good ta play with, an' now ya throw him back like scraps! Like a bone ta an ol' dog!"

"Scraps? I didn't even get a mouthful! If he came home stripped, it wasn't me!"

It was not easy for me to concentrate on what she was saying; however, I did pick up a few of her claims: her husband was to be vaccinated for rabies because of me, I was financially responsible, and was not to escape into thin air. At this point, I fell to the ground for her hold on my throat was depriving me not only of words, but of oxygen. She withdrew my wallet from my red vinyl handbag and extracted my student identification card from it. Something about it quelled her instantaneously. I noticed her thumb touching her fingertips until she was convinced of a number. She glimpsed at the fifty dollars I intended to spend, but did not separate me from it.

"Delinquent," she kicked me before crossing the street as an old man peddled by, flag high on his three-wheeler like a proud tail.

CHAPTER 23

I studied the shelf with care before making my choice: tarragon, allspice, capsicum, celery salt, grains of paradise, bay leaves, caraway seeds, juniper, mace, turmeric, coriander, garlic powder, oregano, nutmeg, cardamom, thyme, cloves, saffron, cumin, paprika, red pepper, thyme, sesame seeds, and dried parsley. I avoided looking at the cashier. I looked down at my bare and blistered feet instead. She rang the small bottles up and, one by one, rolled them down to the bag boy. I could feel her eyeing me like I was weird; maybe it was my teeth chattering, or my shifting from foot to foot.

When I returned, the hob was beaming with anticipation. The idea of cooking was succulent to me. I tore off my hair dress. It stuck to me and I felt like I was skinning myself. My whole body was perspiring, which proved useful, for the spices adhered more easily. I powdered my self instinctively, primitively, powerfully.

When I sat on the hob, the heat was like a magnet attracting my skin, adhering to it so thoroughly, it felt like being sucked into the metal disc. I did not scream, only my other self did, for it was weak just as flesh is known to be. I smelt meat quite soon, several meats at that, for sitting as I was, I'd offered the hob all seven, and as many different skins. The small triangles of fattiness at the junction of my thighs were most unlike the leanness of the red meats; the stringy, brown loop to the back yielded an earthy scent I could clearly distinguish from the buttery, lardy layer of the buttocks; the mild cheesiness of the labia, the fishiness of the mucous membranes, the warm, eggy, yeasty gases that came from the life-giving orifice were each quite unique. I had detected the particular aroma of fish, fowl, red meat, rabbit, pork, veal, and shellfish, when unfortunately the bouquet was spoilt by the smell of burning hairs. These were like onions, put in the pan too early, and now scorching, overpowering the dish. The snapping and popping were not everywhere uniform. Those dangling flaps which can be spread like a tiny quail's wings, whose edges were already crinkly like bacon, strangely, reacted the least, stuck too sadly to the burner to move, they turned a greyish-white. My buttocks, the most sedate of the mass, on the contrary, made a tremendous fuss. The tiny pockets of air behind the dented orange skin were liable to unexpected explosions, and the onslaught of greasiness threatened fire. My intimate folds shrunk before my very eyes. My juices ran down the front of the stove and onto the floor, between the other burners and down my legs and feet; some of it cooked as soon as it was freed, thickened, browned, blackened. The pain was atrocious, for my uncooked cells were still imbued with that force, pulling themselves away from inert food, holding tightly onto the miracle, the autonomy, the fuss, one calls life.

My head, heavy with thoughts, drooped dangerously towards the floor. I noticed a small flame had taken in the triangle of coarse hairs; it was dancing its everlasting hip-thrusting dance, celebrating its power to transform flesh to meat, life to food, pain to senselessness. The kitchen began to turn faster and faster. My head fell forwards, bringing the rest of my body down with it, down onto a pile of dirty dishes which broke, their fragments sticking into the last of me.